Stonewall Inn Mysteries

Keith Kahla, General Editor

By Mark Richard Zubro

The "Tom and Scott" Mysteries

A Simple Suburban Murder
Why Isn't Becky Twitchell Dead?
The Only Good Priest
The Principal Cause of Death
An Echo of Death
Rust on the Razor

The "Paul Turner" Mysteries

Sorry Now?
Political Poison
Another Dead Teenager

Rust
on
the
Razor

Mark Richard Zubro

Mark Richard Zubro

St. Martin's Press
New York

Library of Congress Cataloging-in-Publication Data

Zubro, Mark Richard.
    Rust on the Razor : a Tom and Scott mystery / Mark Richard Zubro
        p. cm.
      ISBN 0-312-15644-8
          1. Carpenter, Scott (Fictitious character)—Fiction.
      2. Mason, Tom (Fictitious character)—Fiction. 3. Baseball players—Illinois—Chicago—Fiction. 4. Gay men—Illinois—Chicago—Fiction. 5. Murder—Georgia—Fiction. I. Title.
      PS3576.U225R87   1996
      813'.54—dc20   96-4244
                                                                    CIP
First Stonewall Inn Edition: July 1997

10   9   8   7   6   5   4   3   2   1

*To the brave and kind
gay and lesbian people in the South
who spoke honestly and frankly to me*

◤◂ Acknowledgments ▸◥

For their kind help and assistance: Barb D'Amato, Hugh Holton, Rick Paul, Kathy Pakieser-Reed, Mike Kushner, Mike Rockwell, and Paul Varnell

If growing up is painful for the Southern Black girl, being aware of her displacement is the rust on the razor that threatens the throat. It is an unnecessary insult.

—Maya Angelou,
I Know Why the Caged Bird Sings

1

Scott trudged into the bedroom, nodded at me, then plodded to the closet, slowly took off his suit coat, and began carefully undoing his tie. Each fold of blue silk took its own meticulous movement to unravel. He draped it carefully on his tie rack.

No question that his meeting had gone poorly.

The more enraged he becomes, the more painstaking his movements. If an opposing batter fears a fastball in his ear, he need only time the lengthening seconds between Scott's pitches. Many a surprised batter had flinched from the following curveball that gently drifted over the outside corner of the plate. Scott might be furious, but he kept control of himself. Then again, a few well-prepared players had found themselves sprawled on their asses in the batter's box.

Scott pulled his white shirt out of his pants, unbuttoned it, and let it hang open over the soft blond down on his chest. Then he sat on the edge of the bed and leaned over to unlace his shoes.

"I'm exhausted," he said. It was only eleven A.M.

We'd talked most of the night before. He'd gotten up at six to be at a breakfast meeting with his agent, his lawyer, and the lawyers from Physically Fit Sportswear, the clothes of champions.

"What happened?" I asked.

"I watched them attempt to pick apart my life. They canceled all the contracts."

He placed the shoes next to each other under a corner of the bed and then draped one black sock over each one.

"They can do that?"

"They did it."

Rumors about Scott's sexual orientation had swirled for months in the tawdry gossip papers. Then, several weeks ago, we had insisted that an attack on us be reported as a hate crime against gay people. The news percolated through the athletic grapevine, but sports reporters in the major papers had hesitated to write about it.

Scott's being gay became national headlines last week, after a speech by Albert Hollis at the Southern Christians for Jesus, Morality, and the Family convention. The Reverend Hollis, from Scott's hometown in Georgia, had chosen to use him as an example of immorality. Without specifically stating Scott was gay, he'd dragged Scott's name through a mire of innuendo. The tabloid press went nuts, with enormous lurid headlines, and ugly rumors flooded through the mainstream press. Other preachers took up the throb of viciousness. Then a friendly journalist in Atlanta called Scott with the rumor that Hollis planned to release a negative video about Scott. Several days of investigation confirmed that Hollis had put together a hatchet job. One of the tamer sections showed clips of my lover autographing baseballs for kids, while a voice-over talked about gay people trying to recruit little children.

Three days ago, Scott had called a press conference to publicly announce his sexual orientation. A sensation followed and still continued. Unfortunately, at practice the morning of the announcement, he'd pulled a groin muscle while running wind sprints in the outfield. He had been X-rayed, examined, and placed on the fifteen-day disabled list. Scott had gone ahead with the press conference. The team decided silence equals safety and said nothing. Officially they didn't have to take a stand, and with Scott out of action, they felt they could delay dealing with the issue of his sexuality. Now, rumors of an imminent trade or involuntary retirement swirled throughout the baseball world.

Most of his teammates with half a brain had figured out he was gay a long time ago. Those who were friends and important to Scott knew and accepted the two of us. At the major-league level, with the high degree of ability demanded of players today, there was little time or inclination for massive prejudice. His close friends on the team called and offered support. Many others said nothing. A few of them made comments distancing themselves.

On the sports radio call-in shows, the idiots monopolized the phone lines, with everything from snickers to outright slander. Usually the hosts cut off the outright threats. I feared for Scott's safety. All it would take was one crazy.

His toughest moment would come after his muscle healed: pitching in front of thousands of possibly hostile fans.

"Are you going to fight them about canceling the contract?"

"I don't know."

I wanted him to say something Churchillian, or I was willing to say it for him—anything that would rally the world to his cause. Something on the order of "We'll fight in every courtroom, carry our cause to the highest level, fight on the beaches and the hedgerows, stand and not be beaten." I'd had to face being openly gay and a teacher, so I could understand a great deal of what he was going through. Nevertheless, it was his career and his world in the middle of total upheaval. I couldn't demand a heroic response from him. I would love him and support him no matter what decision he made. I kept silent.

Scott stood up and winced.

"How painful is it today?"

"Bad as ever."

As a kid I'd been secretly titillated when I'd read that an athlete had pulled a groin muscle. I hadn't known exactly what it meant, but I knew it involved something "down there," that was secret, forbidden, and not to be talked about, and, for a little gay kid, therefore enticing and alluring.

"I'll massage it," I said.

Early in our relationship I'd taken several classes in massage and muscle-relaxing techniques. Because of his profession, he was prone to strains and tiredness. Besides, I enjoyed touching his body, and if it helped him and gave him pleasure at the same time, why not? We'd taken some of the courses together, so if I pulled a muscle while working out he could reciprocate.

He hung his pants on a hanger, and then lay on his back on the bed. I knelt next to him and placed my fingertips on his upper thigh. We talked as I began to knead, rub, and massage.

"What'd they say?" I asked.

"That I am an immoral person and not a good example to the youth of America."

"Well, I knew that."

He didn't smile. "They didn't."

"They actually said you were immoral?"

"Direct quote." His body stiffened for a moment as I hit a particularly sore spot. He held his breath, then let it out slowly. A moment later I resumed my ministrations.

"Your lawyers must have said something."

4

"At great length. Made no difference. The bad guys are calling a press conference this afternoon to announce the deal is off." Scott had a ten-million-dollar endorsement deal with Physically Fit, one of the largest sports advertisers in the country.

"We'll have to cut back on chocolate this year," I said. Still no smile.

"I've made safe investments over the years," he said. "We're not going to have to eat gruel and live on the streets, but this pisses me off." He growled deep in his throat. "And the team lawyer just sat there with his finger up his butt and a fatuous smile on his face."

"He was there?"

"Absolutely. Somebody from the commissioner's office, too. He talked for over half an hour about 'the best interests of baseball' and about possible danger to me physically."

"I think about that, too. I'm petrified about the next time you pitch."

"Maybe I won't have to face that. When I'm better, the team, the baseball commissioner, and whoever else wants to butt their nose into somebody else's business have to make a decision."

"Don't they have to honor your contract?"

"They'll probably have to pay me. I don't think that was ever the problem. It's my being openly gay and a baseball player that's the big problem."

I massaged and rubbed him for a while. He shut his eyes. I felt his muscles begin to unknot.

"Did my parents call?" he murmured a few minutes later.

"Not yet."

In the past few days the only person from his family who had called was his sister Mary. She offered support and encouragement. His parents had known he was gay for several years now and had come to Chicago once and met me. But "acceptance" was too positive a word to use for their feelings about his being gay. They had been pleasant when they were here, but Scott had not been home in many years. He used to visit them once a year, without me, but those forays home had tailed off and then stopped altogether. We had not been invited as a couple, and Mary had told us that several of their siblings had let it be known that if Scott came with a lover for a holiday, they would not. We'd invited his mom, dad, and all his brothers and sisters up to Chicago many times, but except for the one visit, his parents had not returned. Mary, her husband, and their kids visited every other year. Scott seldom said anything, but I knew the distance from his family hurt him. Still, he refused to go without me to the family home in Georgia.

"We could go to my high-school reunion now," he said.

"You're not serious?"

"I guess I'm not. But I think it would be great for both of us to be dressed up in tuxes and walk arm in arm into my old high school."

We'd debated extensively about going to his high-school reunion. Each year in Brinard, Georgia, they invited all the graduates back for one big party. Each year's class tried to organize some kind of theme booth or game in the gym or had a special party or get-together. We'd never gone.

This time Scott's class wanted to do a baseball theme booth. The organizers had sent numerous requests to Scott to get him to attend. My feelings about the trip were mixed. Strutting in proudly in the midst of some small-minded, small-town cretins sounded like in-your-face-fun; but marching in the middle of thousands of people in a gay pride parade in a big city is very much different from being openly gay in East Nowhere, Georgia. Since the reunion was usually during the baseball season, we'd never had to make a final decision.

"I hope you're not serious," I said. "You really think we'd be safe? Look at those murders in Mississippi. With every man, woman, and child on the planet reading about you in the headlines, every nut within hundreds of miles will be on the prowl. I don't mean to sound ignorant, and I know you're from there and you know those people, but frankly I wouldn't want to be caught in rural Georgia after dark with the whole countryside knowing we're gay." Visions of *Deliverance* danced in my head. No gay man I knew wanted to be known as gay and in rural Georgia after sunset. That may be prejudiced, but everyone I'd talked to up north felt that way.

"You've said that before, and it's not like that. Besides, every nut in the whole country will be on the alert, not just in the South. I'll be in danger everywhere, and so will you. That's the part I regret. I'd never forgive myself if something happened to you."

"Don't worry about—"

The phone rang. I picked it up, said hello, listened for a minute, and then handed it to Scott. "Ted Koppel for you."

He sat up abruptly. "Are you kidding?"

I put my hand over the receiver. "Sounds like Ted to me, although we don't talk often."

"Give me that." He put the phone to his ear. "Yeah," he grumbled. Then, "Yes, sir, Mr. Koppel." Pause. "Ted."

I wondered how many people talked to Ted Koppel for the first time sitting on their bed wearing only their briefs.

They spoke for a few minutes. I lay on my side, head propped on my fist. "That's not acceptable," Scott said. He listened. "I'm sorry. I don't mean to be difficult, and I'm not making demands. If you don't want me, that's all right, but I won't be on with anybody from the right wing. I know it's your show, but I won't appear with the stupid, the bigoted, or the ignorant. I won't debate my life or my rights with Nazis."

He listened for several minutes. I watched his chest rise and fall. The noontime light through the floor-to-ceiling windows made the golden down on his chest and legs shimmer. "Okay, that sounds fine. I appreciate your understanding." Moments later he hung up.

"That was Ted Koppel," he said.

"Ted stopped calling me. I don't know why."

"He wants you on with me."

"Do what?"

"I said I'd talk to you about it."

"What do you want?"

"For all of this to go away." He lay back down. "I hate every minute of this. Pitching in the World Series was not as much pressure as this."

I gently stroked his chest hair. "You're the first major-league sports star to come out while still active."

"I don't feel brave and noble. I'm more frightened than anything else."

"We'll get through it together."

His nod held no certainty.

"Did you know Koppel was trying to get hold of you?" I asked.

"Biff and the lawyers have been handling all the calls from the talk shows. They've been negotiating." Biff was Scott's agent. "This morning Biff said he thought a couple of them were in the final stages of agreement. I told him it was okay to give them the new number. I think I want to do this one, and I'd like you to be there with me."

"Okay," I said. Normally, I'd have been thrilled out of my mind to be on *Nightline,* but under these circumstances I wasn't sure how excited I was.

The phone rang again.

"If it's the President, I'm busy," Scott said. He leaned back and shut his eyes.

I picked up the phone, said hello, listened for a few seconds, and then said, "I'm sorry, he's busy."

I dodged before Scott could whack me upside the head. It was my oldest brother calling to get an update on the latest happenings. My parents, brothers, and sister had all called saying they would do anything they could to help. I spoke with my brother for a few minutes. Told him the *Nightline* gig was pretty likely. I hung up and a second later the phone rang again.

"Throw the damn thing across the room," Scott said.

I listened for a moment to the soft-voiced drawl at the other end of the line.

I tapped Scott with the phone. "It's your mom. I think something's wrong."

He sat up and took the phone. "Mama?"

He listened for several minutes. "When? . . . Is Nathan or Mary there? . . . I'm on my way. . . . Don't worry. . . . I love you." He hung up.

"What's wrong?"

"Mama was calling from the hospital. Daddy's had a heart attack. They don't know if he's going to live. I have to go home."

"What can I do?"

He hesitated. "Will you come with? I'll need you. If the worst happens or if he gets better, I'd like you to be there."

"Of course I'll come with."

Beastly hot and ghastly humid midwestern summers had never driven me mad with desire to go someplace even more hot and humid. It was mid-June, and we were heading for Georgia and possibly a funeral. Losing a parent, no matter how old you were or what other stresses you're under, takes total precedence in one's life and emotions. Ted Koppel and a budding career on the talk-show circuit could wait. Scott had asked me to come with. He needed me. I would go with him.

2

I made the calls for plane reservations to Atlanta. From there, we had to hire a private service to fly us to Macon, then rent a car for the two-hour drive east to Scott's parents' house.

As we packed, he filled me in on details. "Daddy went out to check the fence along the west side of our farm early this morning. When he didn't come back by ten, Mama got worried. After she found him, she called a neighbor and they brought him to the hospital."

"They didn't call the paramedics?"

"Why wait for them to drive out from town and then drive back? They're pretty far out."

We couldn't get a flight until four. A flurry of phone calls to his brothers and sisters, a few of whom he managed to get hold of, were followed by cancellation of engagements. Since it was the baseball season, his schedule of outside appearances was relatively light. He only needed to drop out of a celebrity golf tournament.

I was already on summer vacation, so I didn't have to worry about work. I called several friends to cancel dinners, a play, and a movie. When Scott is out of town with the team, I catch up with friends. I'd planned to take all of my nephews and nieces to a game to watch Scott pitch. My mother promised to make all the calls to my siblings to explain. "Is there anything else I can do?" she asked.

"Not really."

"It's going to be tough on Scott."

"I know."

"Tell him I care. I love you, Tom. Be careful."

Is there a mom somewhere on the planet who doesn't tell her kid to be careful when he's leaving on a trip?

Just before we left for the airport, around two, Scott checked with the hospital. No change in his father's condition.

The drive out to O'Hare was done by a mad cabby who didn't seem to be bothered by all the construction, but at the airport every clerk seemed to be working at the slowest possible speed. I'd managed to get first-class seats, and once we were settled on the plane, I immersed myself in Barb D'Amato's most recent Cat Marsala mystery, *Hard Christmas*. Scott drummed his fingers, squirmed in his seat, fussed with the earphones, tried to read a book, and read the safety precautions several times. His anxiety did not make the minutes go by any faster.

Somewhere over Tennessee I put my hand on his and said, "We'll do what we can."

"I wish I could do more."

"I know. We'll be there soon."

He sighed. "I barely remember when Grandma and Grandpa died. I was little, and there hasn't been a death in the family since."

"Who was at the hospital today?"

"Mama and Shannon and Nathan. I wanted to get down there, not talk, although now I wish I'd spoken with Mary." Scott and Mary are the two oldest children. He has two younger brothers and one younger sister. All of them are married except Scott and his younger sister. He also has a mass of nephews and nieces, many of whom he hasn't met because of his refusal to return home, but he keeps a special calendar with all their birthdays on it and always sends them gifts. None gets returned but he only gets thank-you notes from Mary's kids. I mentioned to him once that he might think about cutting off the ones who didn't send notes. He said, "I blame the parents, not the kids."

"How do you think they'll respond at a time like this?"

"Mary will be supportive. I don't know about the rest of them. I hope they forget our differences and want to concentrate on helping Daddy and Mama."

I like Mary a lot. She and Scott are very close.

"Headlines like this week's won't help. I don't know how much any of them ever really discussed my sexual orientation. Mary said Mama and Daddy never brought it up. She tried to talk to Hiram once, but he refused to discuss it."

The difference in the acceptance of our sexuality between my family and his had been made more glaring by my family's eager reception of him and the near-total silence from his. Several years ago Hiram, the brother next closest to Scott in age, had written him a letter saying he never wanted to hear from Scott again.

As we neared Atlanta, I watched a huge thunderhead off to the west. Jagged edges of lightning flashed in the distance. "I hope we don't land in that," I said.

He cast a farm boy's eye on it. "I don't think it'll hit for a while," he said.

We landed in sunlight, but by the time we emerged with our baggage, black clouds and bright lightning covered half of the western horizon. I wasn't too keen on the idea of trying to outrace a storm. Luckily, our charter pilot told us that all small craft had been grounded.

I suggested we rent a car. While I filled out forms and played with plastic, Scott called the hospital. There was still no change.

When we stepped outside the airport and into the

humidity, I almost gasped. My shirt immediately clung to my body. This was cloying, clinging dampness that made walking torturous as your clothes tried to stick to every inch of your skin. I'd served in the Marines in Vietnam, and the memory of that burst back into my awareness as we strode through the humid air.

We threw our stuff in the trunk. The first thing I did after I started the car was figure out the air-conditioning. I set it to winter, and in a few minutes the atmosphere in the car approached bearable. The clock in the dashboard actually worked. It was just after eight, and I reset my watch. The vehicle had only twenty miles showing on the odometer. The new-car smell was almost pleasant.

By the time we left the parking lot, the sun had set. The wind was up, and a few minutes after we cleared I-675 on our way south, lightning flashed in the night sky, wind buffeted the car, and fat drops of rain splattered randomly on the windshield.

"Gonna really come down," Scott said.

"At least it'll cool off," I said.

Always cooler after a rain? Wrong again, midwestern boy.

An hour south of Atlanta the rain swept down in torrents for fifteen minutes. An announcer on a Macon radio station told us this bit of downpour would barely dent the drought they were having and was too localized to do the farmers much good. What I saw out the window sure looked like the deluge to me.

During the rain our speed barely rose above forty. We passed through Henry, Butts, and Monroe counties.

Moments after the downpour stopped, I pointed to a salacious advertisement emblazoned on a huge sign on the left side of the road. "Did I just see a scantily clad, full-breasted woman on that billboard announcing 'Adult Delights'?"

"Myrtle's Exotic Café. Been there since I was a kid."

"A billboard like that on the interstate in Georgia? I thought this was the haven of fundamentalism and purity."

"It's heterosexual, so it's okay."

"You're kidding?"

He wasn't.

I lowered my window to enjoy the cool breeze.

"What are you doing?" Scott asked.

Clinging humidity fought with the car's air-conditioning.

"I was going to enjoy the after-storm coolness."

"Not here."

I waved my arm outside the window. I half expected it to move air. I rolled the window up.

"How did you survive summers here?"

"Same way you survived bitter cold Januarys as a kid. We enjoy the mild winters and endure the heat in summer. When you're young, you don't notice so much. Now we turn on air-conditioning. In winter you turn on heaters. Same principle."

"Sort of."

We took the first exit south of Macon and turned east. One of those rental-sign deals with movable letters greeted us at the bottom of the exit. Brighter than the lightning had been, the sign announced: "Jesus Saves— Garage Sale Saturday." A plethora of signs lined the road. A few had bright smiling Georgia peaches; several advertised Vidalia onions; and one hawked something called orange-blossom honey. Assumedly honey made from or with orange blossoms? I asked Scott.

"I always thought it meant honey made from bees that were only allowed to feed on orange blossoms."

"They can do that?"

He shrugged.

We ate at a nearly deserted Shoney's a quarter of a mile from the interstate. The friendly waitress did not recognize Scott. I hadn't said anything on the way down, but I was worried about the recognition issue. We were gay men in rural Georgia, and while I didn't think the Ku Klux Klan would come riding through the night to lynch us, I wasn't all that sure. I'd heard enough horror stories about the religious right and the rural South to make me uncomfortable. The newspaper machine next to the front door of the restaurant had a copy of the *Bibb County Gazette*—"Your Weekly Newspaper." Under a picture of Scott throwing a baseball, the headline read: "Local Sports Star Gay." The photo showed him standing on a baseball mound against a background of high-school bleachers.

After our meal, we drove in darkness with lightning flashing off to our left and far to the north. Trees rose on both sides of us. Unlike the Midwest, where you can see lights in the distance and feel the spaciousness around you when driving through the countryside at night, here the sides of the road were close and impenetrable. Lights shone only in lonely homes located near the road. Through every small town we traversed, I scrupulously observed the speed limit.

I wanted to keep Scott's mind off his father somehow, but I didn't want to fill the night with endless chatter. What was the point? I just hoped we found Scott's father alive.

"Lots of historical markers around," I opined after we'd taken ten minutes to pass through the twenty-five-mile-an-hour speed limit of a county seat.

"Sherman marched through here during the War of Northern Aggression."

"The what?"

"That's what my history teacher called it in high school. She never permitted anyone to call it anything but that in her presence."

"The Civil War?"

"Yeah. Each marker gives details about what troops of

what division and what battalion stayed next to what creek and what hill."

"They want to remember Sherman's march?"

"They want to preserve every fact of anything historical. Winning and losing is another matter."

"Oh."

We journeyed through Bibb, Twiggs, Wilkinson, Washington, and finally into Burr County. I pointed out the Burr County sign to Scott. "They named a place after a famous American traitor?"

"This is Angus Burr, a hero of the American Revolution. Did something noble in saving people from the English someplace on the coast that was not Savannah."

Several miles of silence ensued.

We finally entered the city of Brinard, the county seat and the population center nearest to his parents' farm. A huge banner was draped from the Rexall drugstore to the courthouse welcoming all the returning grads of Jefferson Davis High School. I slowed down, and Scott gave directions to the hospital. On first sight the notable buildings in town were a Waffle House and the undoubtedly equally exotic Huddle House, both of which seemed to be your traditional greasy spoons, while the more modern variety was well represented by McDonald's, Burger King, and Subway. It was well after midnight, and we didn't see anyone in the town. Not a car moving through the flashing stoplights. No one tooling around the courthouse square.

The hospital surprised me. It was a four-story, modern edifice. A lit sign proclaimed the emergency-room entrance. Light from round globes shone on dusty pavement. Insects sang and owls hooted as we hurried in.

"Only hospital for miles around," Scott said as we swung open the doors.

The reception desk was closed. We followed corridors of red brick and yellow tile to the emergency room for directions. A lone nurse sat filling out forms. As we approached, she looked up from her paperwork.

When Scott gave his dad's name, her whole expression changed, but she made no comment. She merely gave us directions, but I saw her reach for the phone as the elevator doors closed behind us.

Scott's dad was in the cardiac care unit. Upstairs we followed the directions on posted signs to the CCU patient/ family lounge, where Scott used a phone to call the actual unit. No one answered. Scott didn't hesitate: he strode purposefully through the doors to the unit. I followed.

None of the nurses was on duty. Most of the rooms were empty. In one cubicle an elderly woman slept peacefully. Outside the last room on the left we saw a sign with "Mr. Carpenter" typed neatly on it.

We entered the room tentatively. Light from the machines hooked up to Scott's dad cast their blue and green light. I saw blips and heard occasional beeps. One machine read out numbers in red numerals that fluctuated between the high sixties and the low seventies. A tube entered one of his father's nostrils; wires were attached to his chest; and an IV ran to his wrist.

Scott stared wide-eyed at the machines. His dad stirred for a moment but did not waken.

I wondered where everybody was.

Scott approached the bed. "Daddy?" he whispered. "Daddy?"

The side rails on the bed were up. Scott took his father's hand gently and held it. With his other hand Scott carefully pushed back the sparse gray hair on his father's head. A few moments later his father's eyes opened. Scott whispered, "I love you, Daddy."

"Scottie?" his dad murmured.

"I'm here, Daddy."

The man sighed contentedly, closed his eyes, and slept.

Scott leaned awkwardly over the rail and hugged the sleeping figure.

He pulled up a straight-back chair next to the bed and sat in it while holding his father's hand. He stayed like that for the longest time. I stood in the background, unwilling to break the passing of time with words or gestures.

Abruptly, a male nurse appeared in the doorway, saw me, and shattered the serenity of the moment by demanding, "What are you doing here?"

"Singing opera arias," I said. Somehow, when faced with officiousness, I have a tendency to give smart-ass answers.

He spoke with a southern drawl—as did everybody. I'm not going to keep mentioning it; you can assume they did because everybody had an accent. Even Scott's got more pronounced the longer we stayed.

Scott stirred and the nurse took note of him.

"Who are you two?" the nurse asked. "You can't be here."

Scott walked over to us. We both towered over the man, who seemed to be in his late twenties. He had a small mustache and a rounded belly that bulged under his white uniform.

"I'm Scott Carpenter. This is my father."

"Oh."

"The sign in the lounge said visiting in cardiac care could happen anytime, but no one answered our call."

"I was on break."

"Isn't someone supposed to be on duty all the time in cardiac care?" I asked.

"We only have two patients."

"While my father is here, it won't happen again," Scott said very quietly. "I don't know where my family is, but one of us will be here from now on, and so will someone from the hospital staff. I'll talk to your supervisor in the morning."

"You're trying to bully me."

"If my father dies because of any kind of neglect, the least of your worries will be the lawsuit with which I will take every penny you could possibly earn for the rest of your life."

The nurse glanced around the room with his eyes finally coming to rest on me. "Is he part of the family?" he asked Scott.

"He's Tom Mason. He's my lover," Scott said. "He'll stay if I want him."

"Not if the supervisor says he can't. Only family in here."

"Where is everybody?" Scott asked.

"Mrs. Carpenter and her daughter went to the machines in the cafeteria to get some coffee a while ago. I thought I'd be back before they returned. I'm sorry. I apologize. Still, the only people allowed in cardiac care are immediate family. When your mother and sister return, he'll have to leave."

I could see Scott preparing to be stubborn. I didn't want a fight, but I wanted to do whatever I could for him. The phone buzzed on the nurse's desk. He hurried the eight feet to answer it. He listened for a minute and then said, "Only two at a time."

In a minute Scott's mom entered the room. She leaned on Scott's sister Mary's arm. Scott hurried to her, and they embraced.

"It's good to see you, son. So good." Mary hugged the two of them simultaneously. His mother gave me a warm smile and patted my arm. Mary thanked me for coming.

"What's happening, Mama?" Scott asked.

"You can't all be here," the nurse said.

"What needs to happen," Scott said, "is for me to get a status report from my family, and if necessary, from available medical personnel, which I assume is you, and you are going to be very helpful and pleasant."

The nurse hesitated. Scott turned to his mother and sister. "Any news?"

They shook their heads. "They want him to rest. The doctors won't be sure for a while what to do. They may want to operate. They don't know how much damage has been done to his heart."

"He recognized me," Scott said.

"He hasn't wakened," Mary said.

"It was just for a second."

"Is that good?" Mrs. Carpenter asked the nurse.

He shrugged. "You'll have to ask the doctor in the morning."

"You okay, Mama?" Scott asked. "Shouldn't you be home trying to get some sleep? Mary and I can stay tonight. Tom will drive you home."

She smiled at her son. "Your father and I haven't been apart a night in forty years. I'll stay for a little bit. I slept for a while earlier, and I can nap on the couch in the waiting room if necessary."

"I just got here a bit ago," Mary said. "I'll stay. Shannon and Nathan were here all day."

I melted into the background as they discussed logistics, which son or daughter would be expected and when, who was keeping which parts of the family informed.

"Do you have a place to stay?" Mary asked.

We shook our heads.

She offered her home.

"You're too crowded as it is," Mrs. Carpenter said. "And you're too far away. They will stay at the house with me and your daddy."

Scott spent the rest of the night sitting with his dad. I stayed with him for brief intervals. Mostly, I read my book or counted holes in the tile of the ceiling of the waiting room. Once I escorted Mrs. Carpenter to the lounge for a nap. I chatted with Mary for half an hour in the hall and brought up orange juice, candy bars, moon pies, and RC cola from the machines in the basement, depending on who wanted what when. Around four, three teenagers spent half an hour on the waiting-room pay phone making frantic calls. A nurse came and led them away to another part of the hospital.

An hour after dawn, the nurses' shift changed. I was half-dozing next to Mary when three people entered the waiting room. Mary introduced them as Hiram, who'd written the nasty letter, and Shannon, a sister of Scott's. The third was a woman in her sixties, Sally, a distant cousin.

Sally nodded to me. Hiram and Shannon ignored my outstretched hand. They both had Scott's piercing blue eyes. Hiram was in a gray polyester suit. Shannon wore a long-sleeve light-peach blouse and a calf-length dark-green skirt. She wore absolutely no makeup.

Scott joined us. "The doctor's here. We can meet with him." I held back, but Scott took my arm and said, "You come too."

We met his mother in the hall and entered a conference room, full of furniture made of blond wood.

After we were all seated the doctor said, "I just examined Mr. Carpenter." The doctor was an attractive man in his mid-thirties. He had a small mustache, a slight stoop, a thin torso, and the most wonderful green eyes, which looked carefully at each of us as he spoke.

"We admitted him because he was having the signs and symptoms of having a heart attack. He will be in the cardiac care unit while we monitor him and give him some blood tests. We won't know anything for sure for a day or two, until we get some of the tests back. We have to find out how much damage has been done. At times a person with mild symptoms has massive damage; sometimes it is the reverse."

"Will he need an operation?" Mrs. Carpenter asked.

"We'll have to see after the tests are in."

"He's not that old," Shannon said. "He's always been healthy. Why him?"

"No one has an answer to that," the doctor said.

After the conference, it was agreed that Hiram would take Shannon and the cousin home. They would come back later. Mrs. Carpenter and Mary would keep watch in the hospital.

Scott said, "I'd like to grab some breakfast and then come back here for a while. Then we'll go to the house."

We walked down to the cafeteria. Scott looked at the watery eggs and stale toast at the breakfast buffet, gazed around at the white-clad hospital workers, and said, "This is more hospital than I need right now."

We strolled the two blocks to the Waffle House to eat. As soon as we left the air-conditioned hospital, the humidity struck.

"Doesn't it cool off at night or in the mornings?" I asked.

"Some," Scott said.

I breathed deeply. "Fresh pine," I said.

"We're halfway in the middle of the Jefferson National Forest. Jefferson National Swamp is five miles that way." He pointed east.

I eyed the towering trees that lined the street and met above our heads. I knew some were pines and others hard-woods, but that's as good as my botany gets.

The headline on the *Burr County Clarion* outside the Waffle House said, "High School Hero Queer." I stuck a quarter in and bought a paper. I paid for the two that were left in the stack and tossed them in a pink plastic trash can inside the door.

Patrons filled half the booths at the restaurant. A row of men sat along a counter. Most of them wore T-shirts or flannel shirts with cut-off sleeves revealing burly biceps. I felt like a stranger walking into a bar in an old western. All talk stopped. All eyes followed us. A waitress in a beehive hairdo and, I swear to God, with a pencil sticking out of her hair said, "Sit anywheres you want."

We picked a booth that looked out on the passing traffic. Across the street sat a huge old house with graying paint, several pillars at an angle, and a porch that needed propping up. I couldn't see anything through its windows. Everything in the restaurant except, I hoped, the food seemed to be made of plastic: chairs, table, salt and pepper shakers, cash register. Even the menus were covered with it.

The waitress seemed to take an inordinate amount of time to arrive at our table for our order. When she showed up, she smiled shyly at Scott. "You don't remember me," she said to him.

He smiled at her. "Tell me your name."

"I'm Louise Bottoms. I was a year behind you in school. I'm sorry about your dad."

"Thanks," Scott said.

She filled our coffee cups.

I'd never been in a Waffle House, so I ordered a waffle. Always go with the house specialty, I figure. Scott ordered biscuits and gravy. The waitress left. A glance around the restaurant showed me most faces quickly averted, some boldly staring, and a few with studied indifference.

"You okay?" I asked.

"I'm not sure." Scott rubbed his hands over his face, then looked at me. "I didn't know what I'd do when I saw my daddy. It feels so strange. I hoped my mama would be there. I love both my parents, but it's tough. I guess you always figure you'll be the one to bury your parents, but

24

sitting there last night was . . ." He sipped his coffee. "Mostly I remembered stuff from when I was a kid. He used to always take us fishing—nearly every Saturday, when it wasn't planting or harvest. You could go fishing almost every weekend. I remembered the first time he held me in his lap and showed me how to put a worm on a hook. He was patient and gentle. I felt warm and safe and honored for being with my daddy in a quiet and peaceful world only he and I shared. I think I remember the song of every bird, the murmur of every fly, and the water as it touched the banks of the stream. I was the oldest boy, and he was still young and strong. The night before that first trip, I was so excited I couldn't sleep. I must have been four or five."

I gave him an encouraging murmur. If remembering helped, I would listen for hours. He rarely talked about when he was a kid.

"I remember he used to sing us to sleep when we were scared. Oh, yeah. . . ." He gazed off into the distance. Scott began to sing softly the words from "Jimmy Crack Corn." He stopped when tears began to run down his cheeks.

I reached for his hand and covered it with mine. "You're going to be okay," I said.

I heard someone clear his or her throat. I looked up. Louise was there with orange juice, water, silverware, and napkins. She was staring at our clasped hands as if they were a live rattler squirming toward her. I noted that a good chunk of the other patrons must have witnessed my gesture of affection. I squeezed Scott's hand gently and slowly removed my hand. What was there to hide? If the local paper had made our sexuality front-page news, what was the problem? Everybody knew. A gesture I wouldn't hesitate to make in Chicago was now fraught with significance. If people could radiate collective waves of disapproval, this crowd did.

I glanced at Scott. He wiped his tears and blew his nose.

He didn't need extra aggravation at a time like this. I decided I had best watch my behavior very carefully.

From the back of the room a man in a police uniform stood up. He swaggered toward us. I figured it was a good thing that he wasn't wearing mirrored sunglasses indoors.

He stopped at our table. Louise hustled herself off.

He was maybe six-three and might have been an athlete at one time. His paunch protruded several inches over his belt, and the gun, flashlight, ticket book, and handcuffs around his waist seemed to drag his pants to the point of slipping off. His shirt stretched tightly across broad shoulders as well as around his bulging belly. Perhaps if I'd been standing, I wouldn't have felt as intimidated.

He waited for Scott to finish blowing his nose.

"Morning, Scott," he said.

"Morning, Peter," Scott said. "Good to see you."

"I'm sheriff now."

"I heard."

Peter, the sheriff, placed two huge hands on either side of our table. "I won't have any of that faggot shit in here or in this town. No holding hands or anything else. You keep your lifestyle out of here. This is not going to happen while I'm in charge."

His voice carried. If I thought it was quiet when we walked in, now I didn't hear a whisper of conversation. The grill ignored us and spat bacon grease; maybe *it* wasn't prejudiced. Louise dropped a dish; the clatter seemed to rattle and echo forever. Her fellow waitress shushed her.

"If I can, I'll run you and your faggot buddy out of town."

I desperately wanted to go berserk. I rose from the booth. It flashed through my head that this was America, and I was a law-abiding person. I remembered snatches of patriotic blather about living in a great democracy and being equal. But more immediately, Scott was in pain, his father might die any moment, and here was this bully.

I heard Scott saying, "Tom, sit down. Come on, Peter, we were friends when we were kids."

I ignored him. I did not shove Peter, the sheriff, but my movement caused him to step back. I tried to keep my voice calm. I could feel my lips quivering, and I had to draw deep breaths between nearly every word to keep from completely losing control. I said, "We haven't done anything wrong. You need to leave us alone. We're just here having breakfast. Please go away." Maybe that sounds wimpy to you, but it scared the hell out of me to be defying this guy.

The sheriff began to shout, but I didn't stop speaking. "We have broken no laws," I said. "We have committed no crimes. We are here because his father is ill. You will leave us alone."

His shouts had something to do with him being the sheriff and he'd arrest my Yankee ass and no snot-nosed northern scum was going to come into his town and flaunt their faggot lifestyle.

Scott said things like, "Come on, Peter, ease up."

I finished talking and the sheriff stopped bellowing at about the same time. We stared at each other. It dawned on me that while my words might be brave, it might have been a whole lot brighter of me to have kept my mouth shut. Visions of dank southern jails and rabid mobs of angry people seized my imagination. Maybe if I got to know the people, I wouldn't be so prejudiced. Or maybe they were all as big a buffoon as this moron. Our verbiage spent for the moment, we stood breathing like critters rattling antlers at each other, waiting to bang our heads together.

Peter did not look at all ready to ease anything. I stepped back a pace, hunched my shoulders, and clenched my fists, ready for the physical assault I felt sure would come.

Several patrons scuttled out the door. Many gaped in fascination. At the farthest booth from the door, a woman in a white silk blouse and a gray skirt stood up and strode to us. She planted herself between the sheriff and me.

Before we could resume hostilities, she said, "Peter, you are making a fool of yourself. If they do something wrong, by all means arrest them. At the moment they're facing what you and I and all of us are going to face, the death of our parents."

Peter started to speak.

She held up her hand. "Go home, Peter. Go to the police station. Go on patrol. Leave them alone."

Peter drew himself up and glanced around the restaurant. Patrons quickly stuck their faces back in their meals. "You two better watch yourselves while you're in town," he said. "You do the slightest thing wrong, and I'll lock up your faggot asses." He adjusted the bill of his cap, tugged at his belt, and swaggered to the door. He shoved it open, marched to his car, yanked open the door, and started the car with a roar. Tires squealing, he flew out of the parking lot.

◄ 3 ►

The woman who'd confronted the sheriff was a foot shorter than I was. Her gray hair clung in tight curls to her forehead. She slipped a pair of gold-rim glasses from her face and let them dangle on a slender gold chain.

"Thank you for your help," I said.

She gave me a tight-lipped smile and turned to Scott. "I hope your father has a full recovery." She marched out of the restaurant.

Louise returned with a tray filled with our orders. She placed each item on the table in rapid succession.

"Who was that?" I asked Scott.

"Clara Thorton."

"Why did she intervene?"

"I don't know."

Louise leaned over and whispered, "She's the county commissioner. She doesn't like Sheriff Woodall."

"Why not?" I asked.

"I have to get my other orders." Louise fled.

"County commissioner must be all-powerful," I said. "I wonder what hold she has on him. Do you know her?"

"Vaguely. I remember her husband more. He was the town pharmacist when I was a kid."

"I hope we don't have trouble from Peter Woodall. You knew each other?"

"Oh, yeah. Peter and I went through grade and high school together. We were close friends for many years. He was always at my house and stayed over a lot. He wanted a pro career as a football player, and if that didn't work, he'd take baseball. Thought he was pretty hot shit, but he didn't want to pay the price, do all the hard work. Thought he was a natural, and he did have a lot of talent, but he didn't get either career. Got himself elected sheriff couple of elections ago."

"Was he this big of an asshole as a kid?"

"Aren't most kids assholes sometimes?"

"I don't think I want whimsical philosophy. I want cheap, tawdry gossip."

Scott ate a few bites of his breakfast and sipped at his orange juice. Finally he said, "The goofiest thing he and I did as kids was build a raft and try and cross Jefferson Swamp with it."

"Why was that goofy?"

"There's no current. The water just sits there. The only thing that happened was the damn raft kept sinking. Water isn't all that deep most places in the swamp, except when it rains. Lots of very unpleasant snakes, though."

"Always wanted a snake-filled swamp in my neighborhood."

"For weeks, the summer we made our raft, we were filthy and muddy every day when we got home. I got used to sneaking in, changing clothes, and doing my own laundry to hide it from Mama."

"Seems kind of more innocent and wholesome than goofy."

"You ever spend hours chopping down anemic, innocent trees and trying to tie them together with scraps of rope stolen from your dad's barn?"

"I led a swamp-deprived childhood. We built forts in a vacant lot."

"For two weeks Peter and I had canteens filled with water that never lasted long enough. We had peanut-butter-and-jelly sandwiches that got soaked in vile swamp water every day because of our ineptitude. We had planned to sail on a great adventure. We never got two feet."

"Don't all kids make plans for great adventures or have wild dreams and fantasies?"

"And what was yours?"

I ate some of the warm and not overly greasy waffles and bacon. I glanced at my watch. "Shouldn't we be getting back to the hospital?"

"You're ashamed and embarrassed to say what you did."

"I'm not ashamed and embarrassed."

He grinned for the first time since his mother called. "This is Scott you're talking to."

"I'm a little ashamed and embarrassed. I'll tell you later. I'm finished. Let's go."

We walked back to the hospital. I was in a blue button-down shirt and khaki pants, both of which were wrinkled from wearing them overnight. Scott was in gray dress pants and a white shirt that also looked slept in. We both needed shaves. I could have used a shower. I yawned. "We both need sleep," I said. "If your dad's okay, we better think about it."

He nodded.

At the hospital the nurse told us there had been no change in his father's condition. We talked to Scott's sister and mom for a few minutes. Scott stopped in to see his dad. He came back out to say that he was sleeping peacefully. Since we'd been awake the longest, it was decided that we'd go get some sleep and come back early that afternoon. At that time there would be a large family conference.

Outside in the cloying heat I asked, "Are we really going to stay at your parents' house?"

"Mama said it was okay. Why not? It's the house I grew up in."

I'd always wanted to see that. He'd been to my parents' place millions of times. I wanted to know everything about where he grew up and what he did when he was a kid—memories and secrets about the person you love. Before today I'd never had a chance to be in his hometown and this could be my only one.

Scott drove us out a two-lane highway east of Brinard.

"I thought you bought your mom and dad a new house in Wascaloosa, Alabama."

"I did. Wascaloosa's daddy's hometown. They didn't like it. They lived there a couple years, then moved back to the old place. Shannon kept the old place exactly as it was. I paid for any improvements they asked for in the old house. It's got central air-conditioning that cost more to install than it would have to build them a whole new house."

"Air-conditioning is a good thing."

"New plumbing and new electric, too."

"Tell me you didn't have to use an outhouse as a kid."

"I didn't have to use an outhouse as a kid."

We passed a school complex. A three-story red brick building with long rectangular windows stood in the center of several acres. It looked like it had been there since the American Revolution. Several one- and two-story structures surrounded it, including a larger building with no windows, which I took to be a gymnasium. I saw a running track and a stadium open at both ends, with two sets of concrete bleachers running along the longer sides. In the distance was a baseball field with lights and a small grandstand.

I pointed. "Is that where you went to high school?"

"Grade school, everything. That's the ball field I played on since I was a little kid. Under those stands was where thirteen- and fourteen-year-olds would sneak to smoke during lunch."

"Where'd the older kids go?"

"They had cars, the woods, or more important things to do. I can still picture the first time I hit a home run on that field."

"You remember that?"

"Absolutely. I must have been twelve. I was so scrawny, my uniform draped on my body."

"But you still had muscles?"

"I was lucky. Tall and thin, but strong. It was after school on a Thursday, our first game of the season, against Eugenia Junior High School in Filmore County. That's just south of here. We were losing about fifteen to one. I hit the ball just over the left-field fence. Everybody cheered as if we'd won the game. Still lost by ten runs."

"When did you start pitching and stop hitting?"

"I always pitched, but when you're a kid and you're good, they try and get you to play all the time. Even when it wasn't baseball season, I remember pitching and practicing for hours. We didn't have lights back then. We'd play until it got too black to see the ball. We tried flashlights once. Didn't work." He smiled. "I'll never forget the time one of the other fathers got really mad, because in one game when I was fourteen, I struck out all the other kids. Big, ugly old guy in bib overalls, kind of a snaggle tooth."

"He did not."

"Okay, no overalls and no tooth, but the rest is true. I think he wore a white shirt and tie. Anyway, the guy said it wasn't fair and that I should have a handicap. My daddy and him got into a fistfight."

"Anybody get arrested or sued?"

"That's not the way we settled arguments back then. It was just a fight. Only a couple punches got thrown. The other guy had to be helped away. My daddy wasn't going to let some fool hurt his son's chances for fame."

"Must have been great being a star in a small town."

"I never thought about it much as a kid. I was so good from an early age. It's not arrogance, it's just some people are lucky enough to be born gifted athletes, the way that some people are real smart. I knew I was better, I guess. Stuff that was hard for other kids came easy for me."

We were passing through mostly green countryside. Occasional patches of unwonted brown field testified to the drought the rain the night before had not relieved.

"This reminds me of the road to our place in Wisconsin," I said. "Not real flat countryside—lots of evergreen trees mixed in with the hardwoods."

"I guess it isn't much different, 'cept for the lack of snow in the winter."

Past a pig farm on the outskirts of town was a complex of gleaming buildings fronted by a red brick church with soaring steeple. "Reverend Hollis's church," Scott said.

I stared at the lush green lawn even now being watered by sprinklers scattered throughout the vast sward sloping to the road. It didn't look like fire and brimstone.

We passed a trailer park. An old couple sat on corroded aluminum chairs on a small slab in front of the first unit facing the road. Their eyes followed our movement past, but I doubted if anything besides the Second Coming rolling directly in front of them would have gotten them to move. Dirt roads occasionally led off to the right or the left. Despite the drought sometimes I glimpsed ponds of water standing in the distance.

As we drove over a small rise Scott said, "You can see the house there a little bit."

I followed his finger to the left and saw a red roof amid green foliage. Minutes later we pulled onto a dirt road that Scott took for a half a mile. Then he pulled onto a driveway that went maybe fifty feet to a clearing. The house was an unremarkable two-story, almost block-shaped affair. We parked on what I would have called the front lawn.

After he turned the engine off, the first thing I noticed was the incredible quiet. You couldn't hear a passing car, train, or plane. I stood for a minute taking in the morning heat, the totally green surroundings, and then began to pick out small noises: birds in the trees, a dog barking some distance off, the wind as it brushed against the leaves. I could smell woods, and dirt, and freshness.

One long porch ran along the entire front of the house. The screens looked new, and the flower-print covers on the lawn furniture inside gleamed brightly.

To the left and twenty feet behind the house was a barn. Past it were three smaller buildings that looked in need of repair. In the distance was a field of more than five acres with lush green something growing in it. Being from the Midwest I recognize corn and wheat and, in a pinch, soybean. This wasn't any of them.

I tapped Scott on the shoulder. "What's growing in that field? Molasses? Sorghum? Sugar cane? Okra? Drought doesn't seem to have affected it. Sure looks good. Do your parents have irrigation? What is it?"

Scott glanced that way for a second and said, "Weeds." Who knew?

He said, "Don't need much irrigation in Georgia."

To the right of the house as you faced it was a small orchard, which I presumed contained peach trees. I'd seen about a million signs already advertising Georgia peaches. About ten feet to the right of the house was a jumble of car parts surrounding an old Chevy pickup missing the windshield and a left front tire. Next to it was a Toyota truck, sides dirt-encrusted, but windshield intact and tires where they belonged.

"You grew up here?"

"I was born here."

"Do you have a key?"

"Mama and Daddy haven't ever locked up."

We entered through the front door and stepped into a huge space that stretched the entire length of the right side of the house. Toward the front it was a living room, with a brown couch and unmatched chairs of varying kinds, all well stuffed and topped with doilies. Behind this was a massive dining-room table made of thick wood and polished to a shine. Ten sturdy, matching chairs surrounded it. An armoire and a chifforobe, both dark mahogany and highly polished, stood against the walls on either side of the table. Behind this was a gigantic kitchen. Doors to our left were closed.

"Where's your room?"

"Upstairs. All the kids slept up there. Mama and Daddy slept down here. Who'd want to be near all those kids?"

We took our suitcases up with us. The stairs were wooden, with a carpet running down the center. We passed down a hall to the last door on the left. I followed him in. Two twin beds lay against opposite walls. Framed schedules from four high-school baseball seasons hung on the wall above the bed on the left. Half the barn was visible through a window. On each side of the opening were framed pages of the Chicago papers from the days Scott won his World Series games. To the right of the door were a closet and two small dressers.

"Who'd you share your room with?"

"Always somebody. Most of the time I had to share with Nathan, the youngest. You'll meet him later. He has the next farm over. Shannon is the only one who still lives at home. She has her own room up front. When we were kids, she and Mary shared one room, and Hiram and I shared another until Nathan was born."

"Where's the john?"

"Door just to the right of the stairs. All of us had to share that."

"I can imagine the fights."

"And you would be right. I'm going to get some sleep."

He stripped to his shorts and flopped onto the bed on the left. The man can sleep anywhere, and this was the room he grew up in. I left my underwear on and sat on the bed on the right. I let my eyes rove over the interior. I was tired, but my curiosity was aroused. It was like getting a chance to learn the intimate little details of somebody's life you'd always been curious about but never had gotten a chance to know. I pictured all the times he must have come home from school, or from baseball practice, tossing his equipment in this corner or his clothes in the middle of the floor. I quickly corrected myself as I saw his neatly folded pants and carefully arranged shirt. He'd probably put everything away where it belonged. Then again, maybe he hadn't been a neatnik all his life.

Small figures on the dresser closer to the door caught my attention: a set of miniature soldiers in Confederate uniforms. They stood, knelt, or lay in battle poses, guns thrust forward. No blue-coated figures opposed them. I picked one up. It was coolly metallic.

"Will you put that down, lie down, and go to sleep?"

I jumped at his voice breaking the hush. The only sound I'd heard in the house was the minimal thrum of an expensive and well-installed air-conditioning system.

I turned to him. He hadn't raised his head.

"You're awful noisy," he said.

I lay down and stared at the ceiling and surprised myself by drifting off to sleep.

* * *

I awoke to find Scott's open suitcase on his bed, but no Scott. I pulled out clean underwear, another pair of pants, and a clean shirt from my suitcase. I threw on some socks and shoes and hurried downstairs. I found Scott putting out peanut butter and jelly and bread. All the appliances in the kitchen gleamed and sparkled. Besides five feet of counter space on either side of the stove and sink, there were a refrigerator and a freezer, three ovens, including a built-in microwave, and a dishwasher.

"What time is it?" I asked.

"We slept about four hours. It's a little after one."

"How come some of this stuff is totally modern and a bunch of it looks left over from before the Civil War?"

"Daddy likes to keep the old stuff. Mama lets him pretty much, but she insists on having anything new that makes her work easier."

Footsteps sounded outside the back door. It swung open a few moments later. A man who could have been Scott's twin, except for being maybe five or six years younger, raised blue eyes at us.

"Hello, Scott," he said. He took off work boots, opened a door that showed a washing machine inside, stuck the boots on a mat, and shut the door.

Scott introduced us. This was Nathan. We shook hands.

"Any news on Daddy?" Nathan asked.

"I called a few minutes ago. Still not good, but he's no worse."

Nathan nodded. "Y'all staying here?"

"Yeah," Scott said.

Nathan nodded again. "Mama know that?"

"Yes."

Nathan nodded. If nodding noncommittally were a virtue, Nathan would be a saint. You hate to make comments about in-laws, but maybe he didn't have a whole lot of other responses to the world. At least he didn't scream, "Get out, get out, you faggots!"—always a plus.

Nathan said, "Wanted to get some chores done today before I went in. Probably drive to the hospital this afternoon."

"You can come with us," Scott offered.

"Better take my own truck. Don't know what'll happen and who'll want to stay."

He declined lunch and left the room. Minutes later I heard water running. "I could use a shower too," I said. After we ate, I climbed into the most ultramodern shower I'd ever enjoyed. From the outside this might be an old farmhouse, but inside, a lot of it was as up-to-date and well-appointed as any place I'd been in.

We returned to the hospital an hour later. Six Carpenters and I listened to the doctor murmur uncertainties and theories. No one had said a word about my being there, and most often my presence was ignored. I said nothing during the discussions and did my best fade-into-the-background act.

Scott and Shannon agreed to keep watch first while Hiram, Nathan, and Mary took Mrs. Carpenter home to get some real sleep. Mary would return later.

I found a comfortable place on a couch in the waiting room and finished the D'Amato book. If it hadn't been so good, I'd have gotten more of a nap.

I woke at seven and called into the CCU. No change in Mr. Carpenter's condition. Hiram showed up and replaced Shannon. Mary came down the hall. She had the same freckles Scott did along the bridge of her nose. She wore a minimum of makeup and wore her hair straight to the sides with a slight twist on the ends.

After she checked on her dad, she asked, "Why don't we get dinner?"

"Someplace besides the Waffle House," I said.

She laughed. "I'll take you to Della's Bar-b-que. Best place in town. I had a long nap at Mama's, and I could use a walk. I'll show you the town."

It was three short blocks to the courthouse square. On the way I explained what Clara Thorton had done at the Waffle House and asked what her story was.

"Old Clara's a dear. Her husband was county commissioner for ages way back when."

"Scott said he was the pharmacist."

"He did that part-time. The rest of the time he ran the county."

"You mean there's a county commission like the one in Cobb County that was in the news for all that homophobic crap?" Not long before, Cobb County had passed an anti-gay ordinance. One commissioner's daughter had come out of the closet and opposed her father. Hadn't seemed to change his mind. I can't imagine a parent being in favor of denying their own kid basic rights.

"We don't have quite the same setup in Burr County. You may have read about the Supreme Court case a year or so ago. It said that Georgia counties could have a one-person form of government. Black people had sued, saying that type of government kept them from being represented."

"Didn't hear about it."

"In Burr County it's sort of as if there was a president of the county but with no legislature."

"Oh."

"Well, anyway, Clara's husband died, and all the good old boys couldn't agree among themselves who would be the commissioner until they could hold an election. They compromised on Clara, and she's gotten herself re-elected twice now. They can't get rid of her."

"A new southern woman?"

"Only sort of. She actually does most of what the old guard would have wanted. She's been pretty sensible mostly, although she's had some problems. That incident with Peter Woodall wasn't the first. Normally in the South we avoid any kind of confrontation, any open unpleasantness. We can see all we want, but if we keep our mouths shut and don't mention something, then it doesn't exist. At the very least, we don't mention it in public."

"I understand the concept of not scaring the horses, although that does sound hypocritical."

We walked down the east side of the street, across from the courthouse.

"I suppose it is, sort of," she said, "but it's the way we are. We'd rather not mention something."

"Sheriff didn't seem to mind being publicly nasty to us."

"You broke a taboo. You were two guys holding hands in public."

"Scott was hurting. It was an innocent gesture."

"You might as well have blasted a fanfare. You must have seen the headlines in the local papers."

I nodded.

"My brother is the biggest thing that's ever happened to this town. You can't imagine what it was like when he was a kid. Besides being a sports star, he was the most handsome and popular boy in town. He never let it go to his head. Was always kind of shy. All the girls wanted to date him and all the boys wanted to be his friend. People in town would give him stuff."

"Give him stuff?"

"Like free meals when he was out with a date."

"He dated?"

"Of course. He never told you?"

"Only that he went out some."

"Every weekend. Dated the prettiest cheerleader for his entire senior year."

"What was that like for you and your brothers and sister? Lot of jealousy?"

"I loved it, but I'm his older sister. I could get more dates because of him. Sometimes we'd double-date. He didn't like to show it, but he was smart too, but you know that. We'd have these long discussions. You know, the kind kids have about their dreams. We'd sit on our porch on hot summer nights and talk for hours. Those are my favorite memories from childhood."

"How about the younger kids?"

"He brought so much positive attention to the family, I think everybody kind of reveled in it. Hiram tried to be like him. Nathan was sort of Scott's pet, followed him around everywhere. Scott was the hero. The town's connection with fame and immortality. So when the news hit about you two, it hit big. Lots of people feel betrayed. Preachers mentioned it from several pulpits, from what I heard."

"So when I touched him . . ."

"I knew before you got back to the hospital that you two guys had been holding hands. The only way two guys can hold hands in this town is if they're football players in a huddle in the stadium on Saturday night, and that's it. You struck a very tender nerve. And Peter . . . well, Peter and Scott go way back."

"I thought they were friends."

"But rivals too."

"Scott didn't mention that."

"Scott is such a sweetheart. I don't think he notices a lot of stuff like that. He always wants to think the best of people."

We walked past the Rexall drugstore, the First Bank of Brinard, Brinard Hardware, Brinard Auto Parts, and Nellie's Antiques. The sun was beginning to set, but heat radiated off the pavement. The long shadows seemed gentle.

"But there must be gay people in town," I said.

"But it isn't talked about. I've lived in Macon for years, so I don't know specifically about Brinard. I do know that if a man lives by himself, he is referred to as a 'bachelor.' If he doesn't want to be hassled, he goes to Atlanta to have a relationship. Two women might be able to live together, but they'd be harassed on the streets by men trying to date them. The heterosexual southern male mind assumes a woman alone is theirs."

"That's not just in the South."

"If someone was gay in town, it simply would not be mentioned in polite society. Two men openly living together would be close to impossible. They'd have to lie or be closeted in some way."

"Makes horrible sense."

The two-story courthouse sat in its square across the street from us. Immense trees shaded the red brick edifice.

"Is that a statue of a Confederate soldier?"

Mary followed my gaze. "Every courthouse square in the South has one of those."

"Last night I saw the markers about Sherman's march through here."

"Burned most of the farms in the county. Wrecked the town but didn't burn all of it. There's a story of a few of the local women attempting to hide with their valuables in a hollow down by the river, but they were found and lost everything. Most people fled. If you get time, you should visit the Historical Society."

"What happened to your farm?"

"It was Mama's great-grandfather's back then. He'd gone off to war along with his brothers. Only one of them came back. The farm was burned to the ground; all the animals were stolen. Every bit of food was lost to the invaders."

"Do they still call it the War of Northern Aggression in schools?"

"Scott told you that?"

"Yeah."

"Not so much anymore. More years pass and more people move here from the North. The South does change."

A woman in spike heels, a very short skirt, and a white see-through blouse approached us. Her eyes raked me from feet to head, lingering on my crotch. She hesitated as she neared me, gave me a warm smile, and walked on.

"Who was that?" I asked.

"Violet Burnside. The cheerleader Scott dated his senior year."

"She wears that outfit quite well."

"Violet works hard on creating an impression."

Della's Bar-b-que was on the northeast corner of the square. We entered a dimly lit room with booths down the left side, tables in the middle all set for four people, and the kitchen on the right. Almost every table was crammed with noisy revelers. Mary was greeted with friendly waves and expressions of concern for her parents. I felt eyes giving me cool appraisals. She introduced me; people smiled, but said little beyond what was required by politeness.

"Is there such a big crowd because of everybody going to the reunion?" I asked.

"It's one of the big social events of the year. Most people will go. It'll be this big bash in the high-school gym, where too many people will get drunk, and some people will have happy memories."

"If your father is well enough for Scott to take some time away, I'd like to go to the reunion with Scott."

She shook her head. "I don't know if this town, or any like it in the South, is ready for that yet."

The hostess seated us in a booth near the back. I wondered if this was accidental, but then decided I was getting paranoid.

A ham hand landed on Mary's shoulder. The massive fist

of bulging flesh belonged to an overweight man, about five feet eight, in pink knit pants, a white belt, and a yellow shirt with the words "Al's Bowling Alley—Open Every Day" emblazoned across the front. His gleaming smile matched his outfit for brightness.

"Sorry about your dad," he said. "Heard Scott's back in town."

Mary thanked him for the sentiment and introduced me to Al Holcomb. He smiled ingratiatingly.

He did not own the local used-car dealership, as I'd suspected, but I was close. He owned an insurance agency. Al leaned over toward me and confided, "I've been to college up in Kentucky. I'm not prejudiced like these other people. Don't like it when these homosexuals parade around, but I don't mind 'em as friends. I knew one in college. A nice guy. Did a great drag show. He was real popular." I kept myself from thanking him or hitting him.

The waitress taking our order briefly stopped his largesse. When she was gone, he switched topics to talk cheerfully and at some length about how great it was that Mr. Carpenter was fully insured.

Mary looked pained when Al started and awful as he got going. He seemed oblivious. Finally I said, "We need to eat and get back to the hospital. Perhaps later we can talk about it."

After several glad hands and guffaws, he left.

"Who the hell was that?" I asked quietly.

"Al is the head of the local Ku Klux Klan."

I turned to get another look at him. I felt a shiver as I saw him sitting at a table with four children under the age of twelve and a woman in a polyester outfit in different shades of pink.

"He doesn't look frightening. How do you know he's the head of the Klan?"

"We may all be too polite to mention things in public,

but we all know each other's secrets."

I discovered eating bar-b-que meant having pork ribs smothered in a thick sauce. They were the best I'd ever eaten. When we finished dinner, we stood on the sidewalk outside Della's for a minute. Lights from store windows nudged at the night. A police car cruised past us slowly.

"Was that the sheriff?" I asked.

Mary squinted toward the car. "Couldn't tell."

The vehicle continued north and then pulled in front of a building with three other cop cars parked in front. Two bright floodlights illumined the parking lot. The building itself was two and a half stories of dark red brick matching that of the courthouse. Across the street from where the car pulled to a halt was a squat beige brick building with barred windows on either side of the front door.

I pointed. "What is that?"

"Burr County Jail and Eyesore."

"It looks like the kind of place where they had a lynching just last night."

"Hasn't been one of those in decades," she said.

I stared at the building a few minutes. Beyond it a sward of grass studded with enormous trees and soft streetlights sloped down to a small stream.

Mary said, "We better get back."

"It's always this humid, isn't it?" I asked as we retraced our steps.

"It's usually worse. We haven't had a lot of rain this year."

"Don't hurricanes come through here?"

She laughed. "We're too far from the coast. We get lots of rain, but we don't have to evacuate. Supposed to be a big storm coming in from the Gulf in the next twenty-four hours. Farmers are hoping."

* * *

The hall outside the CCU was a bedlam of activity. Nathan and Shannon were near tears. Hiram talked anxiously into the phone.

"What's wrong?" Mary asked. "Is he . . . ?"

"We aren't sure," Shannon said. "They called and said to get here. They said he had another attack. We don't know what's happening."

Minutes later Scott appeared in the hallway. He addressed us all. "Daddy's heart monitor went into an arrhythmia; he had more severe chest pain. They're going to do an angioplasty to try and clear any blockages. It could kill him, but if they don't do it he'll probably die."

"Should we move him to a bigger hospital?" Hiram asked.

"Burr County General has everything a big city hospital would have," Nathan said.

"It's a hick town with barely enough facilities," Shannon said.

They looked at Scott, who looked at Mary. "If he should have been moved, it's too late now," Scott said.

"Dr. McLarty is a heart specialist," Mary said. "They put the hospital here so it could serve several counties. This one specializes in cardiac cases. The one two counties over has all the experts on diabetes. They divided it up like that all over this part of Georgia. An Atlanta hospital might be able to specialize in a lot of these, but we've got just as up-to-date heart facilities right here. It's the best around."

"It's pointless to fight and second-guess," Scott said. "He's getting the best care. We'll just have to wait."

The hours barely moved by. Fortunately I'd brought Carolyn Hart's *Dead Man's Island* as a backup to the D'Amato book. I barely looked up at the passing scene. Siblings paced; more cousins and in-laws appeared and disappeared. Scott insisted his mother lie down.

After nine Scott and I took a break outside the doors of the hospital. No traffic passed on the street. Bugs began to sample our skin. I told him about dinner and the people I'd seen and met.

"You saw old Violet?" he asked.

"Yeah. You really dated her?"

"For more than a year."

"I believe the polite term for her appearance would be 'voluptuous.' "

"She hasn't changed much. She was nice and smart, though. Lot of that was an act."

"Did you . . . ?" I hesitated.

"Did I what?"

"You and Violet."

I got a shot of blue-eyed amusement. "Do you really want to know?"

I shrugged. "I guess not." Actually I did, but some things are best left unsaid (and probably unasked).

We went back upstairs for more waiting. Around eleven I walked down to the food machines in the basement.

I took the stairs instead of the elevator. It would take more time and give me a little exercise. As I strode down the silent corridor, I heard soft voices ahead, already at the machines. When I heard my name, I slowed down. I caught the middle of a conversation.

"You mean Mama said they could stay in the house?"

"That's what Scott said. I think his buddy slept in my old bed."

"How can she let him bring that fag into the house? Somebody's going to have to talk to them."

"Who? You're next to Scott in age."

"But you were always closest to him. You were his pet. You're the youngest. He won't get mad at you, or if he does, he won't hit you."

"He wouldn't hit you. Anyway, you're big enough now to fight back."

"I wouldn't want Mama to know we were fighting at a time like this. He *has* hit me. Remember the time in high school?"

"You were kids, and you did leave his favorite baseball mitt at the park along with his lucky bat, and they both got stolen because of you."

"How many times do I have to say it wasn't my fault?"

"Scott blamed you."

"And beat the shit out of me."

"I thought Daddy was going to beat the shit out of him."

"He didn't, though. He always did like Scott best."

"Will you give it a rest? We have to decide what to do about him going around town with that faggot. Did you hear what happened at the Waffle House this morning?"

"The whole county knows and half the people between here and Atlanta. I wish the sheriff could run that queer out of town. I'd beat the shit out of him myself if I wasn't afraid of Scott."

I decided I'd heard enough. I stepped back a few paces in the hall and then walked forward making loud sounds with my feet. The voices stopped. I rounded the corner and smiled at Hiram and Nathan. Their bland faces revealed nothing about the mayhem they'd been contemplating. They said nothing as I inserted coins in the machine, punched my selection, and retrieved my RC cola. I smiled at them and left. They kept silent as I walked away.

Back upstairs, I read for a while and then began to doze when, around midnight, Scott whispered to the family who were there. "The doctor's back."

I stood next to Scott as the family gathered in the hallway. Dr. McLarty took off his green cap and wiped his forehead. He spoke directly to Mrs. Carpenter. "The procedure itself was a success. We've cleared as much of any blockages as we could find. We still don't know the extent of the damage that has been done. We've done what we could, but we just won't know for a while. Time will have to pass. He is breathing on his own, which is good."

"Can we see him?" Hiram asked.

"You can sit up with him, but you can't speak with him. And only two at a time."

"Mama?" Scott said.

"I'll go," Mrs. Carpenter said. "You come with me, Scottie."

The remaining brothers and sisters discussed their father until Scott and his mother returned half an hour later.

"Mama should go home," Scott said quietly. Mrs. Carpenter looked gray and tired. She made no protest.

"I'll take her," Mary said.

They discussed familial logistics. It was unlikely Mr. Carpenter would awaken before morning. All of them were tired, but Scott insisted he wanted to stay. I volunteered to stick with him. Hiram and Shannon began to protest at that, but Mrs. Carpenter said, "I think that's a good idea. Scott and Tom should stay. We'll all be fresher in the morning."

"How'd your dad look?" I asked as we watched his family leave.

He shook his head.

"How are you holding up? You haven't had much sleep in the past few days."

"I'm okay. I'm awfully glad you came with."

We reentered his father's room. Scott sat next to the bed and held his dad's hand. I sat in a chair and read.

As the first hints of gray dawn appeared Scott said, "I want to stay here for a while. Can you go back to the house? Maybe get my shaving equipment, change of underwear? I don't want to leave."

"You should get some sleep."

"I want to be here if he wakes up."

"I'll stay if you want."

"Bring me back that stuff," he said. "I need you now as I never have before." We hugged. I could feel his tension as I held his shoulders.

"I'll be back as soon as I can," I said.

"You remember the way?" Scott asked.

"As long as it's daylight, I should be okay. The turnoff from the highway is the first left after the second crumbling gas station?"

"Yeah."

"And it's the third dirt road on the left?"

"On the right."

No nurse was on duty as I left the CCU. I walked down the muted and empty corridors and this time took the elevator down. The hospital doors swung open automatically. I stood in the entrance for a few minutes, stretching my arms. I realized I'd left my book upstairs. I turned to go back, but then figured I'd be back in a while anyway. The air was damp and almost cool. Tendrils of fog drifted about four feet above my head. The nearly empty parking lot looked eerie: clear visibility at ground level, and then these wisps of fog, and then above them a dark sky to the west but faint grays and the first blues off to the east.

I ambled to the car. The lights in the parking lot flicked off as I approached our rental. I saw a dark figure in the backseat of the car. "Now what?" I muttered.

As I approached, the bulk didn't move. A few seconds later I was close enough to recognize, despite the deep shadows, the grinning face of Peter Woodall, the sheriff. I unlocked the front door and flipped the lock for all the doors. An unpleasant odor mixed with the new-car smell. I guessed it had something to do with the nearby forests, swamps, and farms. Odd I hadn't noticed it when I walked out of the hospital. Maybe the wind had changed.

By the time I wrenched open the back door, I'd completely lost my temper. "I don't know what the fuck you think you're doing, you son of a bitch. I've never done anything to you. I just want to be left alone. As soon as Scott's father is better, we're leaving. I wouldn't want to stay in your goddamn county anyway."

Woodall just kept staring forward and grinning.

"Look, asshole," I continued, "maybe you've got some score to settle with Scott. Maybe you should fight a duel or do whatever it is macho guys do in the South, but why don't you leave us the hell alone until that can be arranged?"

He grinned some more.

I leaned further in. Most of his body was shrouded in darkness. The odd smell was almost overwhelming. "Look, shit-for-brains, maybe you can hide in the backseat of people's cars in this part of the country, but—"

The grinning face slowly leaned toward me and then continued past my startled expression and slumped all the way over.

I grabbed the body before it could fall out of the car. It was cold. The front of Woodall's shirt felt damp and sticky. "Shit."

I shifted his bulk so he was sitting up. The light was dim, and I could still barely see. I looked at my hand. The sticky dampness I'd felt was blood.

I lifted Woodall's head up to feel for the carotid artery, although I figured it was quite useless. I'd held dead bodies in the jungles of Vietnam, and this one felt just like those. Checking the carotid was indeed pointless. Moving his head gave me the cause of his death. His throat had been slit.

4

I'm afraid that the vision that flashed across my mind was that of my father. One Saturday afternoon he was showing my brothers and me how to fix something on his car. He'd just toggled some switch or other and started the car when a puff of smoke and a tongue of flame rose from inside the engine. My father stood there for a minute. We boys backed away a few steps, wondering if the car or my father would explode. He just stood there with his hands at his side, staring into the engine. All he said was, "This is a revoltin' development."

My sentiments exactly.

I looked at the body. I held out my blood-covered hands. With nothing to wipe them on I tried using the floor of the car as the nearest dry surface. I got most of it off, but stray smears and small patches of stickiness remained. Touching the body had also gotten blood on the front of my shirt and pants.

I looked around to see if there was anyone in the vicinity to call to for help.

Nobody. I didn't need to be involved in a murder investigation in the South. Who knew what lunacy might be perpetrated?

I hesitated to go for help. The only other person who

had been here was the murderer. The crime scene could hardly be more pure or better preserved. With the light at hand I did some examining. Woodall's shirt was bloody, but the car itself had very little blood on it. With that kind of wound more than his shirt would have gotten soaked; the area around the body would be saturated. The pavement surrounding the car had no visible signs of blood, either. Obviously, he'd been killed somewhere else and brought to this spot. Why our car? To implicate me? Scott? Both of us? Or maybe every killer looks for a handy spot to plop a dead body, and our rent-a-car happened to be it.

I didn't see signs of a struggle. His clothes seemed to be in order, not tugged or pulled out; his gun was in its holster, his hands lay by his side, and I couldn't see any signs of abrasions or bruising. Whoever did it either was very clever—maybe drugged him—or was powerful enough to hold him still with one hand while slitting his throat with the other. A very powerful person—or several people. Of course, there could be all kinds of signs of restraint that I missed. I ran my hand along the floor, then under and on the seat as well as under the sheriff. I found nothing.

I looked back toward the hospital. As yet no one had emerged onto the parking lot. It was at the back of the hospital, away from the street, although I doubted if much traffic existed anywhere in Brinard in the early morning hours. Even now I heard no sound of activity. There were two other cars within a hundred feet of this one and another clump of cars closer to the street. I presumed these belonged to the hospital workers. Possibly we hadn't been singled out. Maybe the killer or killers had simply picked this one because it was farthest from any light.

I wished I could just get in the car, take the body, and dump it off the nearest bridge. I presumed no one had seen the murderer but half the town would be on hand to see me try to surreptitiously slip the body into the nearest swamp.

I sighed. There really wasn't much else to do. I walked back into the emergency-room entrance.

The nurse saw the blood on my clothes and jumped to her feet.

"I'm fine," I said. "The sheriff is in the backseat of a rented white Oldsmobile about two hundred feet from the front door. It probably won't do any good, but you should send some medical personnel out there."

"Why?"

"His throat has been slit."

She swung into action. She pressed a button with one hand and reached for a phone with the other. I stopped in a john down the hall and washed the rest of the blood off my hands. By the time I got outside, the wisps of fog were gone, and it was full daylight.

A blue police car with white lettering saying "Brinard County" sat about ten feet from our car. The cop car had its Mars lights rotating. A blond guy, who fit his brown polyester uniform pants very nicely, stared into the backseat of my rental car. Three white-coated emergency-room workers stood in a clump about five feet from the body.

I joined the cop. He had a lovely blond mustache and short blond hair mostly covered by a brown cap. He might have been in his mid-twenties. He wore a tan shirt that emphasized great pecs. He barely took notice of me but kept staring at the backseat of the car.

I tapped him on the shoulder. He didn't move.

"I found the body," I said.

"Was he dead?" the cop asked.

"When I found him? Yes." I thought it best not to add that "I found the body" implies that it was dead when I discovered it. I was extremely tired, but I wanted to stick with a general policy of quiet cooperation and compliance.

He just kept staring at the body. Since the cop's responses seemed to be limited, I strolled over to the medical people. One woman and two men.

"Shouldn't we try to revive him?" one asked.

"You can tell he's dead."

"I know he's dead."

"We should do something. He's the sheriff. He can't just be dead."

"Can't be much deader."

"Y'all see a point in attaching electrodes, starting transfusions, or inserting IVs? Blood would just flow right out again."

That they could recognize dead when they saw it I thought was a plus.

Another cop car drove up. A very slender, dark-haired guy got out. He seemed to be about the same age and height as the blond.

"What's up, Harvey?" he said to the blond.

Harvey pointed. "Sheriff's dead."

The new guy walked up to the car, opened the back door, lifted the sheriff's head, and whistled. He rejoined Harvey. "He's dead all right."

I was pleased at this new confirmation of the obvious.

"This is gonna be big news," the dark-haired one said. "Every official in the county is gonna want to be in on this one."

I wasn't sure which one I wanted to interrogate me. The dark-haired one's hips were narrow and his shoulders broad, but the blond had lovely muscles. I doubted they'd let me choose.

Mostly I stood around as a crowd gathered and what must have been half the officials in the county examined either the body, the car, the ground, or all of the above, in general doing everything but preserving the integrity of the crime scene. Several herds of demented elephants on their morning stampede couldn't have obscured the evidence any more than these people did.

No one suggested we adjourn to a nice air-conditioned car or building to avoid the heat and humidity, already unpleasant at this hour.

Around ten a lean, grizzled man with dark circles under his eyes drove up. He wore a very light gray suit and tie. His full head of hair was cut short and was totally white.

Everyone stepped back and allowed him space. They waited for him to speak. He barely looked at the backseat of the rental car. The first thing he said was, "Cody, cordon off this area. Move all the people back, including the doctors and nurses." The brown-haired guy moved to obey. So Cody was the name of the slender broad-shouldered one. The older man put his hands on his hips, gazed at the sky, the surrounding buildings, finally the pavement and the car. He saw me and walked over.

"You found the body?"

I hadn't seen anybody tell him. Somehow word got around in this town as if everybody had their own Burr County CNN antenna attached inside their skull.

I nodded.

"I'm Wainwright Richardson, the county coroner." He did not offer his hand to be shaken. "I take over when the sheriff is incapacitated. I'll be handling the investigation. I want you to give your statement to Harvey." He pointed to the blond.

At this moment Scott approached me from across the hospital parking lot.

"How's your dad?" I asked.

"Still breathing on his own. Shannon and Hiram are with him. They told me Peter was dead. What happened?"

"I found the sheriff in the back of our rent-a-car. Rent-a-corpse? Whichever. He was very dead."

Harvey strolled over. I liked the way he hooked his thumbs on either side of his oversized buffalo-head belt buckle. He pointed at me. "I want to talk to you."

"Don't worry about me," I said to Scott. "I'll be fine. Get back to your dad." Scott hesitated. "It's okay," I said. "Everything will be all right."

He still hesitated, but Harvey placed his hand on my elbow, less than a yank but more than gently, and led me toward a cop car.

I was sweating in the morning heat. The parking lot had no shade, and I could already feel warmth from the concrete radiating through my shoes.

We sat in the front seat. He took a hand-sized note pad from the dashboard.

"Can you turn the air-conditioning on?" I asked.

"Listen, faggot, everybody knows what happened yesterday between you and the sheriff. If I can hang this on you, I will."

The towering anger triggered by that kind of unfairness ran smack into my cooperation vow and my good sense. Calm was absolutely essential at this point. I said, "Officer, I'm willing to do anything I can to help. I found the body. I had no reason to kill him. I barely knew him. I've been at the hospital all night. It would help me if you didn't address me as 'faggot.' "

"I don't give a shit what would help you. The sheriff was my coach in high school and my friend. He helped me get this job. He's dead and I'll call you anything I want. Just answer my questions."

"Am I a suspect?"

"Don't start that lawyer shit with me. Just talk. I want everything you did last night in order." He held his hand poised with pen over pad.

So I told him. Just to be nasty, I spent an inordinate amount of time trying to snatch glimpses of his polyester-covered crotch. This is a great way to make a straight man feel uncomfortable. Once he caught my glance and quickly looked away.

By the time we were finished, I'd sweated through the back of my shirt and the seat of my pants. The window on my side faced the east and the sun shone in on me. The open window let in what little breeze there was.

Harvey flipped his notebook shut. "Stay there," he growled. He got out and walked directly to the coroner.

During the interrogation someone had been taking crime-scene photos and another person dusted for fingerprints.

I gazed at the assembled mass of gawkers. More vehicles had arrived, including an ambulance and one more cop car. Twenty-five feet away a crowd of thirty or forty people stood behind yellow crime-scene tape. As each new spectator arrived, the car where the body still sat in the heat was pointed out and then fingers would swing in my direction.

I saw Clara Thorton in earnest conversation with Wainwright Richardson.

Minutes later I spotted Scott trying to enter through the police cordon, but Cody stopped him. No one seemed to be noticing me, so I got out of the car. I strolled over to Scott.

"News on your dad?" I asked.

"I was just upstairs. Nothing. You look miserable."

"I've been sweating in that damn car."

Several officers noticed us and pointed. Cody, Harvey, Clara, and Wainwright moved toward us. The crowd behind the police cordon surged in our direction. I saw teenagers and little kids on bikes, older women in sun hats, young men and women in jeans, and elderly couples in khakis. I guess there isn't an approved gawker-at-tragedy uniform.

I observed the approaching mass of officialdom. "It's the cavalry," I said, "and I don't think they're riding to the rescue."

Over their shoulders I could see Sheriff Woodall's body being placed in a body bag and into an ambulance.

"What's happened so far?" Scott asked.

"I was questioned. They should be done. I never got your stuff from the house."

"No big deal."

When the group of officials arrived, Richardson said, "Mr. Mason, we'll want you to come down to the police station to sign a statement. We also will have a few more questions."

This had gone on just about long enough. I said, "I'll want a lawyer present, and I'll need to make some calls."

The three others looked at Richardson. He gripped his chin in his hand, nodded slowly, and said, "We'll decide that when we get to the station."

I didn't like the sound of that and began a protest. So did Scott, but two cops positioned themselves on either side of me. They didn't cuff me, but I wasn't free to leave, either.

"I'll get you out," Scott called to me.

"Call Todd Bristol," I shouted back. Todd was our lawyer in Chicago. I was beginning to dislike this big-time.

I was placed in the backseat of Cody's police car. He did not turn on the air-conditioning, but the rush of the wind through the open windows as the car moved gave some relief.

I said, "So, Cody, how 'bout them Braves?"

"Shut up, asshole."

Tension-relieving chatter was not Cody's long suit.

The drive of a few blocks took only moments. Cody led me up the steps of the police station. It was two stories tall, with four windows on both sides of the front door. The woodwork around them was painted white. It could have used another coat. Inside, the linoleum floors were faded yellow with black flecks. Pine, stained dark brown, covered the walls halfway to the ceiling; the upper portion was painted pale beige. The first floor was basically one large room with offices around the sides, separated by glass partitions that reached only three-quarters of the way to the ceiling. A reception desk was immediately to the left as I walked in, staffed by a gray-haired woman answering the phone. A low wooden railing separated the reception area from the rest of the fifty-by-fifty-foot space.

Two African-American men in cop uniforms stood off to my left on the far side of the room. Four white people in plainclothes worked at various desks on the other side of the railing. I noticed potted plants and pictures of families on desktops. One desk had a typewriter with a yellow rubber duck on top—it had the friendliest face of anybody or thing in the place.

I was fingerprinted and subjected to paperwork being filled out. All the people talked more slowly than I was used to in Chicago. For a few of them I wanted desperately to reach over and press their fast-forward button. It didn't seem like they'd ever get done speaking. Everyone was reasonably polite, but nobody moved a speck above slow, as if time were theirs to play with. All this took until after twelve. Finally, they led me up stairs that were immediately behind the reception desk. I saw a hallway as dreary as the space below. They put me in the first room on the right.

It was not a suite at the Ritz. The best thing about it was that there were no rats or crawling critters visible. There was a chair, but one of the legs was slightly shorter than the other, which made sitting in it annoying. The table in the center of the room could have been shellacked and made into a shrine to the criminals who had carved their initials, names, what I hoped were nicknames, and obscene graffiti into it. The window had wire mesh on the inside.

Nobody stayed in the room with me. For comfort I finally moved the table against a wall and sat on top of it. I waited and wondered. No doubt in my mind that I was a suspect. I tried the door. Locked. I decided if there was a fire I could batter the table or chair through the mesh on the window and jump two flights down. They hadn't taken my wallet, watch, other valuables, or shoelaces.

There was no air-conditioning and I had no way to remove the wire mesh and open the window to get some fresh air. At first I sweated a fine mist of damp all over my body. Then I started to drip. An hour later, when rivers of moisture were running off me and with my worries mounting, Wainwright Richardson came in.

I neither gave nor got a cheery greeting. He refused my first and all subsequent requests for water. Richardson took the chair, turned it backwards, and straddled it. He had to lean forward so the short chair leg rested on the ground. I guess it doesn't do to rock back and forth while grilling a suspect.

"You're in a lot of trouble," he said.

"I want my lawyer."

"Don't you start that with me. We aren't up north. We take our slow time down here and we do things right."

"If you're doing things right, you're tracking the sheriff's movements from last night, finding out who saw him last, seeing if there were any witnesses for this morning, checking to see who had grudges against him. I want my lawyer."

"You talk a lot for somebody in so much trouble."

"I'm just enchanted with the luxury of the surroundings and the charm of my hosts."

"Why'd you kill him?"

"I want my lawyer."

"Now, we're not getting anywhere this way. You need to talk to me."

"I want my lawyer."

As his questioning continued, my responses didn't vary much from "I want my lawyer" and "I don't know why you keep asking me things—I want my lawyer." Kind of a dull conversation, but I was beginning to move from worried to scared.

After an hour of this I said, "You have nothing to hold me on. I'm leaving."

I got up, walked to the door, and tried the handle. It was still locked.

"You're staying here," he said quietly.

"No, I'm not." But I think he knew my bluster was for naught.

He said, "Your boyfriend may be rich, but down here we take murder seriously. Don't have much crime in this county, and we don't like strangers coming in and causing trouble."

"Are you a throwback?" I asked. "Is this *Mississippi Burning?*"

"What's that?"

"A movie. Look, I know I haven't crossed any international boundaries. You people might not like me because I'm gay, but you must read the papers. The world is changing. You can't just lock somebody up and throw away the key. Eventually there will be lawyers and publicity involved with this."

"We'll handle any problems." He knocked three times on the door. Harvey, the young blond cop, opened it. Richardson slipped out. I didn't bother to rush them. I could see the headline: "Faggot Shot While Trying to Escape."

Sweating before was as nothing now as the heat of the day stretched into late afternoon. Outdoors had been stifling. Inside was beastly. During the next hour, I took my shoes and socks off, let my shirt hang open, and contemplated stripping down to my shorts. For the hour after that, hunger and especially thirst became massively important as I tried to think of all the long cool drinks I'd ever had. The third hour had me in my underwear. I sat on the floor with my back against the wall. I shut my eyes and must have dozed, because I woke with a start as somebody rattled the doorknob. I did not leap to my feet. I wanted a drink of something and didn't care who saw me nearly naked.

The door opened and I thought, this is the end. The man who stood in the door looked like the warden from the movie *Cool Hand Luke,* only this guy must have been in about his sixties. He was a mousy guy with a hat, a short-sleeve shirt, hands on his hips, and an arrogant air. I glanced over his shoulder for a man in mirrored sunglasses who would be toting a shotgun.

I expected him to speak in a reedy-whiny voice, the first words of which would be, "What we've got here is a failure to communicate."

He gazed around the room, caught sight of me on the floor, and said to someone behind him, "Get this man some water, and I want a fan in here now!"

He propped the door open with his briefcase, bent his pudgy frame down next to me, and offered me his hand. "You okay, son?" he asked.

"Think I'll sit until the water gets here," I said.

He nodded and went to the door. A pitcher of water, a glass, and a fan were brought in by a lanky teenager. "Thank you," my savior said. The kid scuttled out.

He poured me water and handed me the glass. I gulped greedily.

"I'm Beauregard Lee," he said. "Call me Beau. I'm a lawyer. I got a call from Todd Bristol. We went to law school together. Don't tell him I told you, but he was my first lover back when dinosaurs ruled the world."

He plugged the fan in and aimed it so the breeze hit me directly. I drained the water from the glass, poured myself another.

"Took me a while, because I had to drive down from Atlanta, and I can't stay long. I've got to get back for a huge case tomorrow, and I don't do criminal law, but Todd said you were a sister, and I know how these backwoods towns can be. The death of the sheriff was on all the news stations."

"I haven't been charged with anything yet."

"Not from lack of trying."

"Huh?" I felt somewhat better. I reached for my pants, stood up, and pulled them on. Beau looked disappointed but didn't comment.

He said, "The only thing these people have done all day is try and tie you to the murder. Every step you and Scott have taken since you got here has been investigated. What they don't have is direct evidence linking you to the murder."

"I didn't do it."

"I understand. They don't. They know you're gay and you're a stranger. You corrupted their favorite son. Led him to Sodom."

"He was more than willing."

"Yes, but they don't want to know that, or won't accept it. The big cities and evil ways have stolen him from them. There is a lot of affection for Scott Carpenter in this town, as you can imagine. I remember as he was growing up reading about him in the Atlanta papers as all-state everything. He was gorgeous then."

"How is he?"

"He's been downstairs most of the afternoon. He's been trying to get to see you."

"How's his dad?"

"I don't know. I told him to go back to the hospital and that I'd call him as soon as something developed here."

"What's going to happen to me?"

"The only thing that's stood in the way of you being arrested, so far as I can tell, is that the district attorney is a young fella just out of law school."

"And he isn't as prejudiced and narrow-minded as these others?"

"He's a part-time preacher at the local Evangelical Christian Reformed Nazarene church."

"That doesn't sound promising."

"He's totally new on the job, which is somewhat good. He doesn't want to be made a fool of in court. He knows he has to have a case. He wants to go exactly by the book, and going by the book at this point for you could be a very good thing."

I stuck my feet in front of the fan and began to pull on my shoes and socks.

"Any chance I'll be let out of here?"

"I should be able to get you out without you being charged. If they find enough evidence to arrest you, that's a whole 'nother thing, as I'm sure you know, but this has been long enough."

It was after five by now. He asked me what had happened from the moment we got to town. I told him. When I finished he said, "Come on with me."

"They wouldn't let me out the door earlier," I said.

"Stick with me."

Beau took me by the elbow and walked me past the young blond cop. Harvey shuffled uneasily but let us pass. He followed us down the stairs. Beau stopped at the bottom of the stairs and gazed across the room at Cody, the dark-haired cop. Beau said nothing, just nodded to himself, and turned to the reception desk.

Violet Burnside was standing near the reception desk. She wore tight short-shorts and a halter top that emphasized her enormous endowments. her hair looked artificially colored, and I thought I saw lines around her eyes that her excessive makeup almost completely concealed.

She was speaking to the receptionist and several men in sport coats. I presumed they were plainclothes cops. She giggled and simpered at them.

Once they noticed us, they all stopped talking.

Wainwright Richardson came out of an office near the back. He strode to the railing. His eyes kept one continuous glare on Beau.

"May we leave?" Beau asked.

"Your client may not leave town. Any attempt to remove him from this jurisdiction will result in his immediate arrest."

"Thank you, Mr. Richardson, I understand. We want to be fully cooperative."

More dagger glares as we left.

Outside, even the humidity felt good for at least the first couple minutes of freedom. We stood in the parking lot.

"What do I do now?" I asked.

"I'm not sure. You're still in danger, and not just because of the murder. You've got more to worry about being prominently gay. Most people in the South are reasonable. However, as anywhere does, we have our share of lunatics. Try not to be in the countryside alone after dark. Carrying a gun is iffy. Do you have one?"

"No. Scott's family might, out at the farm."

"Too long of a wait for a permit for you to carry one. And if you did, it could be an invitation to a nut to open fire—or it could protect you. Course, if they caught you with one without a permit, they could lock you up for that. Try to be with a crowd at all times. You might think of hiring a private detective."

"A local investigator? You're seriously suggesting I trust somebody in this town? Other than you and Scott, there's isn't anybody in hundreds of miles that I would trust."

Beau sighed. "I wish you could leave."

"I wouldn't want to go with Scott's dad being ill."

"Your lover is also in more danger now."

"But we haven't done anything."

"You're a living, breathing, openly gay man, and this is the rural South."

Cody the cop walked out of the station with Violet, who certainly looked like she knew how to get a straight male's testosterone flowing. She stood close to him, her thigh only a small shaft of daylight away from his crotch. She ran a fingernail down his chest and only stopped when it reached his belt buckle. He grinned and she giggled.

"Touching scene," Beau said.

"You stared at him after we came downstairs."

"Any gay man would, but it wasn't just because of that. Either his exact twin or as 'Stud Likely' that man dances every first and third Saturday night at a very exclusive gay men's club in Atlanta. Mr. Likely ends up wearing only a fishnet G-string when he's done stripping."

"He'd make a great Stud Likely."

"I'd say so. I heard Mr. Likely had some mysterious background from a few of my friends who could afford his after-hours services."

"I don't think I'll ask him."

"You might. Somebody had to commit this murder. One handy way of getting yourself off the hook would be finding out who did it. People with secrets are a good place to start."

"Nobody in this town is going to talk to me."

He thought a minute. "I'm afraid you're right."

Violet leaned close to Cody and their lips met. She grinned at him as he swung into a squad car and drove off.

Violet casually gazed around the parking lot, at the windows of the police station, and then sashayed over to a white Cadillac parked three cars from where we stood.

"That's either salvation or deep trouble," Beau said. "Who is she?"

"Scott's girlfriend from high school."

He shook his head. "I'll take you back to the hospital and I'll talk to Scott, but I can't stay. I'll try and get you a reliable lawyer from in town. Doubt if I'll find you a gay one. Until you discover the real killer, you're in deep trouble. More publicity could simply bring out more maniacs from the deep woods, but then a town crawling with reporters makes it tougher to gun you down."

"You think it would come to that?"

"I don't want to think that. I just want you to be prepared and be careful."

Beau walked into the hospital with me. Outside the CCU lounge Scott swept me into his arms in front of Hiram, Nathan, Shannon, and two nurses. Scott's mom and his cousin Sally were in with his dad, who was resting comfortably. In the hallway, away from the family, I told Scott the whole story.

"I shouldn't have brought you here," he said when I finished. "And now you can't leave."

"I'm glad I came," I said. "I want to be here. Whatever you and your family need is what's important to me."

Beau said, "I appreciate your sentiment, but you'll need to do something proactive to find someone else to be the main suspect in this murder. I cannot emphasize how much trouble you are in."

I nodded. I saw Scott staring wide-eyed over my shoulder. Following his gaze, I saw Violet Burnside, clutching a massive purse and swaying her hips seductively, strutting down the hall toward us.

"Violet?" Scott said.

She said nothing. When she reached us, she dropped her purse on the floor, threw her arms around Scott, whispered "Scottie," and planted her lips on my lover's. He put his arms on her shoulders and gently eased her away. He introduced Beau and then me, stating that I was his lover.

She looked me up and down more slowly than she had on the street. "You're very beautiful, both of you." She talked in a high-pitched, breathy voice.

Beau said, "I'm sorry, Miss Burnside, but we have important business to attend to. If you could just give me a few minutes with these two gentlemen . . ."

She sighed, turned so that she faced the three of us in a semicircle. Her sheen of magnolia blossoms and delicacy dropped completely. Her voice was still airy and light, but she pointed at me and said, "I know you're in trouble, and I know your relationship with Scott. I loved Scott and have beautiful memories of his kindness to me. You'll need someone from here to help you out of this situation."

Scott began a protest, but Beau interrupted. "Dangerous and deadly matters are at hand, Miss Burnside. Are you sure you'd want to be involved?"

She smiled at him and I thought she was going to revert to type, but she said, "It's all right. I know very well what I'm doing. Word around town is you're from Atlanta. Will you be able to stay and help?"

"No," Beau admitted.

"Then," Violet said, "by default, I am the rescue team."

5

Nobody had a better solution, and frankly I was feeling desperate. I didn't want just a lawyer to protect me, I wanted an entire platoon of gay commandos in battle fatigues toting machine guns—guys who had been working out in every gym in the country, could bend steel with bare hands, with all the necessary accouterments for stud-rescuers.

Violet said, "Scottie, you want to stay here with your father. I'll bet Tom's hungry."

Her saying it reminded me that I hadn't eaten since some time in the middle of the night, and then only a stale candy bar from a machine in the hospital basement.

"I wanted to have my brothers protect Tom," Scott said. "Nobody would bother you if they were escorting you around town."

"Will they do that?" I asked.

"If I ask them to."

I hadn't told him about the conversation I heard in the basement. I wasn't eager to have the Carpenter boys as my protection. He looked for them, but they had disappeared, and no one knew when they would be back.

Violet touched Scott's arm. "And if Tom comes to my place to eat, we can compare notes about you, Scottie."

After some discussion, Scott gave in, I said okay, and Beau agreed.

Inside her white Cadillac she turned on the engine, set the air-conditioning, picked up a portable phone, and dialed a number. She spoke with a friendly breeziness to whoever answered, then turned to me and said, "What would you like on your pizza?"

"Cheese and sausage," I mumbled.

She spoke the order into the receiver and then hung up. "I hope you weren't expecting a home-cooked southern meal," she said.

"If I don't have to cook it or clean up after, it's gourmet."

She slapped my thigh. "I think I like you."

As she guided the car out of the parking lot, she asked in a very quiet voice, "What's it like living with him?" She glanced at me, then concentrated on negotiating her way through the traffic around the courthouse square.

"He's kind and tender and beautiful," I said. "He has his faults, but I have mine. He would do anything for me, as I would for him."

"He hasn't changed much. As a boy, he was kind and gentle and beautiful. The most handsome boy in three counties. I loved him as only a teenager can love."

"What happened?"

"You're asking me?" She laughed pleasantly. "He was always such a gentleman. I didn't figure it out until years later, when he never came back with a beautiful bride. When we were kids, it was such a joy not having to fight him off, but then I began to want him to at least touch me. It took me forever to get him to go out necking in the woods." She sighed. "He was so sweet."

In minutes, we pulled up to an unprepossessing home on a quiet street eight blocks from the square. The house was red brick along the base and halfway up the first floor and then wood above that to a second story. An enormous screened-in porch ran the length of the front.

In a kitchen bright with geegaws, we sat at a Formica-topped table. On top of the refrigerator, next to a clock radio, was a picture of Violet with a boy who looked to be about twelve. She saw me noticing and said, "That's my son, Scott."

I smiled.

"He's spending the summer with his dad. I ran off with his father when I was nineteen. He was a lean, mean truck driver with blond hair and a ponytail. We were divorced seven years ago. I think of him as my starter husband. I moved back to town last winter when I got a job here."

She poured me a large glass of lemonade, placed the pitcher on a towel near at hand, and sat down next to me. "With any luck he'd be rotting to death in a dismal swamp."

"Sounds miserable."

"The first time he hit me was the last. I grabbed him by the balls and twisted so hard it put him in the hospital. He agreed to a divorce right quick after that. Haven't seen him since, but my son lives with him every summer."

"Why does such a rotten guy get the kid?"

"I have custody, but he gets him on some holidays and parts of summers. A court order is a court order. He gets the kid for every allotted minute and that's all."

The doorbell rang. She left the room and returned with a pizza. I wolfed down a quarter of it before she had eaten one piece.

"Didn't feed you in jail?"

"What was with those guys?"

"Who can ever be sure what is with men? I went down there to find out what I could. The whole town is in an uproar about the sheriff and you two. I wanted to do what I could for Scott. If that means helping you, I will."

"You aren't hoping to win him back?"

She smiled at me. "You're very shrewd. I suppose in my fantasies that crossed my mind, but I believe in reality and doing what can be done. I know he's yours. Even that little while in the hall in the hospital, I could tell how much you love each other."

"And that didn't bother you? You wouldn't want to maybe see me in prison or executed, so you could get him back?"

"Shrewd, careful, and maybe a little paranoid."

"I'm in a fix. If you're going to turn on me, I at least want it out in front that I have these fears."

"Aren't you too paranoid?"

"I've had kids follow me down Clark Street in Chicago screaming 'Faggot,' and that frightened me plenty. I very definitely don't want to be alone in the rural South with somebody screaming 'Faggot' at me. That may be paranoid, but my guess is every gay or lesbian person in America would agree with me. Look at that case in Mississippi where the guy killed two gay men. You know, with the lesbians and that farm."

She nodded.

"They're trying to get a killer off using the 'It's okay to kill them because they're gay' defense."

"Only way those fears about me are going to go away is for me to help you. If it doesn't work, you're no worse off, because—let me tell you—you're very bad off now."

"What does that mean?"

"I need to give you a little history lesson."

"Beau, the lawyer, told me some."

"But you need a local perspective."

I leaned back and munched slowly on another piece of pizza.

"When Scott was growing up, he was the pride of the county. When he was a junior in high school we won the state baseball championship for the first time and then turned around and won it again the next year. Burr County burst with pride. We'd never come close to winning anything in any sport. Atlanta papers sent people to do articles and even put some of us on television. It was the closest we'll ever get to fame, unless a serial killer shows up in town. Anyway, Scott pitched and hit and did everything that made us win. He got his own parade through town. We also made it to the semifinals in football his senior year. He wasn't the main player, but he started at wide receiver. The sheriff, the one you found in your backseat, was the hero of that team. They were best friends for years. I went out with Peter some before I dated Scott."

"How was Peter as a date?"

"Typical. Ordinary. Wrestling matches on Saturday night. Begging me just to touch him. He was nearly as handsome as Scott." She traced her finger around the top of her empty lemonade glass. She sighed. "The point is, this town idolized those boys, and especially Scott. With that big family on their farm, it was just idyllic. He was so masculine and strong. And you see, now all that is gone.

"Sheriff's dead. Scott Carpenter is gay. Since the headlines in the paper, people have claimed that they knew long ago. Sure, there were probably a few rumors over the years since he's been gone. I heard one or two when I moved back, and a few of the more perceptive people in town, if they gave any thought to it, might have figured out he was gay. But most people don't want to know, and now that they know, they aren't happy about it."

She sounded like Beau. I told her what he'd said.

"Sodom brought home on our streets," she said. "I heard the ministers were going to try and get together and have a united front against you both, angry sermons or some protest or other, but Scott's family has a lot of respect in this town. Plus there are those who won't deal with the facts. Even if you two walked through the courthouse square at high noon naked and holding hands, they wouldn't accept that their hero was less than perfect."

"But most people are angry?"

"Yep. Everybody might or might not be sad about the sheriff being dead, but you finding the body is bad news."

"What do you mean, not being sad about him being killed?"

"Sheriffs in small towns know everybody's secrets. That's not any different south or north, east or west. He had enemies."

"Clara Thorton, for one."

"I heard what she did at the Waffle House. I was surprised at old Clara. She's supposed to be the one who encouraged the ministers to organize some kind of protest or statement about you two."

"She must have hated Peter."

"Pretty much."

"I've got to talk to her."

"Sure thing. Of course, I can't see Clara wielding a razor in a blind rage, holding down the sheriff, and slitting his throat." She laughed. "Mad Clara from Georgia."

I told her about what Beau told me about Cody. "I need those kind of secrets."

"I don't know that many of the more recent secrets. I only moved back to town last year. I've been gone too long. But Peter would have known them for sure. He was always furtive for no reason. Kind of a funny kid. Popular enough, but if he hadn't been a sports star, I don't know."

When she paused, I asked, "Don't know what?"

She rubbed her hands against her upper arms. "I think he could have been a brute. He never tried anything with me, but I wonder."

"How about talking to his wife or his kids?"

"Kids are too little. Leota, his wife, was a year behind us

in school. When I dropped him, he started dating her. She became head cheerleader the year after me. We can try."

"Who else in the county? Who would fear him? The rich and powerful?"

"Depends on who had done what, how illegal it was, and how desperate Peter was to get reelected."

"County politics in the South don't have a great reputation."

"And you live in Cook County, Illinois, where the dead vote?"

"Only in really close elections."

She chuckled. "Most political power is in Clara's hands, followed, in no particular order, by the tax commissioner and then the probate judge. Not things you hear about much."

"And sheriff."

"Well, that's up there, too. Course, in the past thirty years we've had federal inspectors in here monitoring the elections more than half the time. African-Americans are a majority on the board of education, but it's still pretty racist here. It's just not brought out in the open. Everything is a secret."

"I'm going to need to know these secrets if I'm going to get out of this."

She glanced at the clock. "You ready to start tonight?"

"I'm pretty beat, but I slept on the floor in the jail for a while. I think we'd better get moving if we can. Where are we going to start?"

"With Cody."

"You were awful friendly with him earlier."

"I find flirting with particular men helpful. A divorced woman is a target for every male who thinks he's the only one who can satisfy her. Once she sees how spectacular he can be, why, then she'll be happy to cook, clean, and slave for him. Her reward is two minutes of pleasure twice a year when he's drunk. If this town thinks Cody's after me, then they leave me alone."

"Maybe it works that way for him too," I said.

She looked at me quizzically; then her face cleared. "I never thought of that. I wanted to start with him, because we're sort of close. Since your lawyer told you about him dancing in Atlanta, he sounds like the best bet."

"Think he killed him?"

"Let's find out."

We slipped through the heat to the car. She drove for a few minutes until we were out of town heading south.

"Aren't you afraid of being seen with me?" I asked.

"It'll be reported around town soon enough. We've got to move quickly and be reasonably discreet."

About five miles out of town she turned onto a dirt road lined with trees whose branches met overhead. "We're going to Rebel Hell, the local pool hall, gambling den, and pickup bar."

"I thought you couldn't get a drink served in the South."

"Depends on where you are and the kind of place. This kind of place will do what the customers want. Cody will be here. All the deputies come out on Wednesday night."

"Out mourning the sheriff's passing?"

"It's a place to be together. They'll mourn him."

"Maybe I shouldn't be with you."

"We've got to talk to him. I'll go in and you'll wait in the car. He'll come out with me. Maybe you better wait in the backseat."

The car bucked and rocked over the ruts and potholes in the dirt road for more than a mile and a half. We stopped in front of a shack maybe fifty feet long and twenty-five feet wide. The parking lot was loose gravel and had three or four cars and at least thirty pickup trucks in it.

Unease lurked at the fine edge of my consciousness.

Could Violet be leading me out here for a convenient lynching? It had been years since she was close to Scott. Maybe this was her chance for revenge. I decided if more than one person came out of the shack heading in my direction, I'd run out of the car and take my chances in the woods.

She seemed to sense my fear, because she leaned over and patted my arm. "It's going to be fine. I'll be out in a few minutes, but I'll leave the keys in the ignition. If you feel uncomfortable, tear out of here fast."

The windows of the bar were wide open. Through the screens I got a clear view inside. If I lived here, I'd have preferred an establishment that kept the windows closed and the air-conditioning on high. I turned the ignition to power, lowered the window on my side from the master control on the driver's side, then flicked the key back off.

I listened to the calls of birds I didn't recognize and crickets and frogs and the hum of insects. Blue-lit electric bug-zappers hung from the opposite corners of the bar's roof overhang. The sound of death zaps punctuated the night air. The noise of the jukebox in the bar reached my ears easily, although Violet had parked as far away from the light as possible. A wall of bushes loomed on my left. Violet had put the car under a tree so it was in even deeper shadow. Through the branches and leaves I could see overhead a nearly full moon shining amid the millions of stars you can't see from the city. Back to nature. How lovely. At the moment, for my money you could pave the entire state of Georgia and turn it into a parking lot.

The minutes passed. I could see Violet inside speaking to a small crowd of men. I thought I caught glimpses of Cody with a cue stick in his hand.

Most of the people I saw inside were white men in jeans and T-shirts, some with logos advertising particular beers, rock groups, or unpleasant things they'd like to do to their enemies. A few women, both black and white, sat at the bar. They wore the same outfits as the men.

Three guys appeared in the screen-door entryway and gazed out at the night. Were they looking toward me? Suddenly one of them burst from the door. He took several steps in my direction, abruptly turned to his right, and ran to the far side of the building. The sounds of him being sick added dissonance to the symphony of the velvet Georgia night. His buddies laughed uproariously, helped him to a dirty brown pickup, and tossed him in the back. They climbed into the cab and left.

The remnants of the air-conditioning had all seeped from the car and I'd begun to sweat. I pulled my back away from the seat and yanked at my already damp shirt. The screen swung open and two guys walked to the opposite side of the parking lot. They swung themselves into a red pickup, turned on the lights, revved the motor, and drove off in a swirl of gravel. What if they were going to block my escape? I became more uneasy.

Violet finally appeared in the doorway with her arm around Cody. The T-shirt that clung to his broad shoulders and enwrapped his slender torso said "Go Tech." His jeans clung to his narrow hips. He nuzzled at her neck but seemed reluctant to leave. Several raucous calls came from inside. These had to do with how lucky Cody was.

I switched the dome light off so it wouldn't come on when the car door opened. I moved silently out of the front and crawled into the backseat. I inched my head up so I could see. I felt childish and stupid crouching around in the middle of the night. Then again, I didn't want to be executed for murder.

Giggling and laughing, they stumbled into the car. Violet started the engine.

"I don't want to go anywhere," Cody said. "Thought we were just going to visit out here."

She patted him and said, "We've got to talk." When she pulled out of the parking lot onto the dirt road, she said, "Tom?"

I sat up.

If Cody was drunk, his reaction didn't show it. In seconds I was looking down the barrel of a gun.

"Put that away, Cody," Violet said. "We just want to talk to you. Where did you get that?"

"Under my shirt in back. I don't go out to Rebel Hell without it. Crowd out here is tough."

"Put it away," she said. "He's not going to hurt you and neither am I."

He lowered the gun a few inches. "What is this bullshit?"

"I didn't kill the sheriff," I said.

"That's what they all say—'I didn't do it.' If your pal didn't have connections, you'd be safely in jail."

"My connections say you dance naked in Atlanta on the first and third Saturdays of every month."

The gun barrel reached much farther up my nostril than I ever thought it would go. I squirmed backwards.

Violet yelled, "Stop that, Cody!"

Cody followed my movement back and was half over the seat. The car swerved violently. Cody lurched off balance for a moment. I grabbed the hand with the gun and smashed it against the roof of the car. I'd had just about enough of fear. If the guy didn't dance, I'd be dead. I smashed the hand again and the gun dropped to the floor of the backseat. I did not pick it up.

Cody was sore. "You mother-fucking son of a bitch, I'll arrest you for resisting arrest, for attacking a police officer, and for kidnapping a cop! Don't think I wouldn't arrest you too, Violet. You won't get away with this."

I said, "I've got directions to the address in Atlanta, Violet. If they recognize him at the dance club, we'll be fine." If not, I thought, we might as well just keep driving until we get to the moon. I suspected kidnapping a Georgia police officer was a crime heavily frowned upon in this jurisdiction.

Violet drove through Brinard and took the road west toward the interstate. We were silent through two counties.

As Violet swung around another courthouse square, Cody said, "You don't have to do this."

In the light from the dash I could see his brown hair and brown eyes and firm jaw. The hand I'd smashed trembled a little. From the pain or from fear?

"Cody, I don't want to hurt you, and I don't want to bring trouble to you. I'd rather not get information or help from you by threats and coercion. I just need help."

"I'm not gay," he said.

"How'd you wind up dancing?" Violet asked.

He was silent a minute and then said, "A buddy from the police academy came down to go hunting with me. He told me about this bar, said the guys who danced made a lot of money from fat old desperate fags. Said at least half the guys who danced there were straight, but did it just for the money and laughs. I guess I asked more questions than most. He wrote the address on a card and said they were very discreet. Deputy sheriff in this county don't pay much. I went up there once and they hired me."

"You didn't have to put out for the owner?" I asked.

"He's straight. It's strictly money to him."

"You let guys paw you. You hug and kiss them in public. They grab your dick, and my source says you charge huge amounts of money for after-hours personal parties. Sounds kind of gay to me."

"I'm straight."

Violet said, "I'm not sure I care who either of you choose to prong on a Saturday night. Question is, did the sheriff know?"

"Or anyone else in town?" I added.

"No."

"Nobody ever mentioned or noticed your frequent and regular trips to Atlanta? Some high-ranking county official like the sheriff didn't stumble into the bar one night, catch you, and threaten to expose you?"

I tried watching his eyes as he answered.

"Nobody I knew ever showed up. I made money, that's all."

"Sheriff didn't get suspicious that you were living beyond your means?" I asked.

"I put the money into an account in a bank in Savannah. I haven't spent any of it yet. I'll use it to buy a decent house when I get married."

"People will wonder how you could afford it," Violet said.

"Maybe I don't plan to live in this town forever."

Violet drove onto the interstate toward Atlanta. Cody stared out the window at the scenery for several minutes.

"Tell me about the sheriff," I said.

"I know you want to try and save your ass," Cody said, "but I think you killed him."

I sighed. "I'm working from the accurate premise that I didn't and I need information. Aren't you at least concerned with justice in this? You dance in a gay nightclub, you can't be as prejudiced as a lot of these people."

"Faggots are pathetic. Pawing at me. Hoping for a little hug back. It's disgusting."

"How nice they tip you," I said.

"Yeah, well."

"We'll keep your pretty face and your prejudices out of the paper if you talk. If not, we may or may not believe you about being straight, but Burr County is going to think you've gone over to the minions of Satan, no matter what the truth is."

He placed his fists against the dashboard and stretched his arms straight. Then he twined his fingers together and cracked his knuckles one by one.

Finally he said, "Sheriff didn't tell his deputies a lot of secrets. Burr County Sheriff's Department runs pretty much like any other small county. We give out traffic tickets, keep teenage rowdiness to a minimum, hassle with domestic disturbances, deal with break-ins and burglaries. County fair is kind of work for a week each year. We've got ten guys full-time, with two black guys to handle crime in the black community. Sheriff goes around with them around election time asking for votes."

"That still happens?" I asked.

They both glanced back at me. "You got a better solution?" Cody asked. "You want white cops going into the black community to make an arrest?"

"Good to know white cops are afraid of something."

"It isn't fear. It's just sensible."

I decided not to debate police-department procedures in the South.

"Tell me about the sheriff."

"Okay to work for. Like any boss, he had his good days and bad."

"What about the bad days?"

"He might chew your ass out for doing something stupid, but if you did your job, he was okay."

"Anybody in the department that he particularly didn't like?"

"Nope. Everybody sort of got along."

"How about in town?"

"Town's pretty peaceful."

"Come on," I said. "Man like that has to have enemies. Who were the tough cases in town? People who had grievances against him."

"Well, we got Jasper Williams. He's sort of the town nut."

"God, yes," Violet said. "He is one crazy bastard."

"How so?"

Cody said, "He's sort of one of them skinhead Nazi types. He's never been to Germany but wants to go real bad. He hates Jews, blacks, and faggots."

"He's not in the Klan?" I asked.

"He's too nuts even for them," Cody said. "He lives about a third of the way into Thomas Jefferson Swamp. Burns crosses in strange rituals on his own property, tortures critters, and tried to dam up the water in the swamp. Built this huge dike that didn't do no good. Water just oozed around it. FBI came down and investigated him a few times. Thought he might be printing hate literature. Found boxes of swastikas. That's how he came to the attention of the sheriff."

"I remember that," Violet said. "He put them down the median strip of the roads around the courthouse square for the Fourth of July last year."

"He was mad when the sheriff locked him up. Threatened to exterminate the whole police force."

"Great," I said. "He killed the sheriff. Lock him up and throw away the key."

"Doubt it. He's got guns out there, and he's threatened just about everybody in town one time or another, but he's never done anything to anybody. He got a piece of mail all messed up in his post-office box one time and claimed he was gonna shoot everybody who worked there."

I leaned forward in the car and Cody turned half-sideways so that we could look at each other while we conversed. He seemed almost like a decent guy giving information.

"You let that kind of nut run around?"

"Never committed a major crime. I do know that some people stumbled on his place accidentally once. Hikers who got lost. Don't know what he did to them, but they hightailed it out of town right quick, claiming they had to escape. They said he had snakes and torture stuff and wouldn't hang around to press charges. I know I wouldn't want him to catch me in the swamp at night."

"I still don't believe you let him run loose."

Cody said, "Doesn't hurt that his daddy is very rich. Lives up north somewheres but still owns a big chunk of the county."

Violet said, "That plus there's a lot of toleration for eccentricity in the South."

"This doesn't sound eccentric to me. I think it's sick."

"He didn't kill the sheriff," Cody said. "Last I knew, Harvey and one of the guys went out to warn him not to light any fires. It's been so dry, even the swamp could go up in flames. They didn't find him, but they left a note."

The young cop might not have Jasper Williams on his suspect list, but ol' Jasper was sure on mine.

"How about Al Holcomb, the one in charge of the Klan?"

"Him and Peter golfed together nearly every Saturday. They've been friends for years."

"Maybe Peter was a Klan member," I said.

"I doubt it," Cody said. "Everybody pretty much knows who's in the Klan. Never heard the sheriff was. Only about fifty people in the whole county are in the Klan. It's not that big a deal."

"How about Clara Thorton?" I asked. "Peter and she had that big blowup in the Waffle House yesterday morning. Everybody saw it. Or maybe somebody used that fight as an excuse, a chance to kill the sheriff and blame it on Clara or us."

"That was just politics between them," Cody said. "I grew up in town, and I know Clara's husband didn't like the sheriff. Never did know why."

"Is that the basis of their disagreement, or is it more recent?" I asked. "There's got to be some reason."

"I know Clara has opposed getting more police officers for years," Cody said. "Me and Harvey only got hired a couple years back because two guys retired. Every time the sheriff tried to get more money for police or anything for the department, she said no. Hasn't been an improvement in years. Cars are getting so bad we couldn't catch a snail in a high-speed chase."

"Yeah," Violet said, "I remember the quote in the newspaper Clara gave. Something about cops don't prevent crime, they just come around after and write reports."

"I'm going to talk to her," I said. "Who else?"

"Before I came into the department, I heard the sheriff almost got into a fistfight with Hiram Carpenter, your buddy's brother."

"I never heard that," Violet said.

"Hiram has a temper," Cody said. "He can be pretty mean. Him and Peter was in Rebel Hell and Hiram was pretty drunk. Guy accidentally bumped into Hiram. Poor guy apologized but Hiram belted him, knocked him out with one punch. Hiram's damn strong. Sheriff told him to go home and Hiram got pissed."

"He didn't get arrested?"

"Naw. It was only a fight. He didn't actually hit the sheriff. He swung and Peter stepped back, grabbed Hiram's arm after the fist went by, and pitched him out the screen door. Hiram charged like a bull, but Peter just turned at the last second, pushed him into the wall of the building head-first. Sort of took the fight out of Hiram. Still took three guys to get him into the back of his pickup."

"That's something," I said.

"That's nothing," Cody said. "That's just a Saturday night at Rebel Hell."

"How'd the sheriff get along with Wainwright Richardson?"

"Never heard of no problems."

We feel silent for several moments. Finally, I said, "Let's go back."

She nodded, took the next exit, and swung back onto the interstate going south.

"Cody," she said, "you're not going to try and do something stupid like talk to people about this?"

"Tell everybody some faggot and a girl dragged me off and threatened me?" He paused. "You're right. I can't have people finding out about what I do. You've got something to hang over my head." He jerked a thumb toward me. "If I can find a way, I'll lock you up, and no threat will stop me."

I thought of giving him the lecture that I was gay, not a faggot, and Violet was a woman, not a girl, but what was the point?

The three of us barely said a word all the way back to Rebel Hell. Violet turned on a country music station. Some of the songs I sort of liked, since I could understand the words. I wasn't sure I'd understood any of the words to rock music since I was twenty-two.

By the time we got back, the parking lot of Rebel Hell was more than half empty.

"Can I have my gun?" Cody asked.

I reached down to the floor, hesitated, then realized it made no difference. Even if I didn't give him his gun, all he had to do was go into the bar and tell his buddies. We probably wouldn't get far.

I handed it to him. He hefted it gingerly, stared at each of us in turn, then slipped it under his T-shirt in back.

"Where to?" Violet asked as I watched Cody's narrow hips as he strode to a red pickup truck. I got in the front seat as he roared out of sight.

"The hospital." It was after midnight. "I want to see how Scott is and get the latest on his dad. I want to talk to some more of these people tomorrow."

"I'll help," she said.

"I appreciate that. You're willing to take off work?"

"I'm the town librarian. I have my MLS and I run the place. I can do what I want."

I looked at her clinging halter top and short shorts.

"You have something to say?" she asked.

"You're intelligent. You're educated. You flirt shamelessly with the men. You dress like Daisy Mae."

She laughed. "What's a nice girl doing with a persona like that?"

"Yeah."

"If I can use my femininity to get my way, I will. I'll do whatever it takes to subdue my world. If I wear a halter top and men drool, I can get more things than if I wear a conservative business suit. For years the library here was scandalously underfunded. Since I've been in charge, allocation has gone up fifty percent. I'm sure it's because of my persuasiveness. If that upsets some women, I don't care. They don't live here and they don't live my life. I take care of myself very well, thank you, with no help from anyone."

"Don't know if I've ever met a librarian quite like you," I said.

She laughed. "I'll call one of the girls to come in and cover for me. Lisa's saving up for college and always wants more hours."

At the hospital she accompanied me to the CCU. Hiram, Sally, and Scott were in the hall. They told us that Scott's dad was still resting comfortably and there was as yet no definitive prognosis.

Scott said, "I slept a few hours earlier. I'm going to stay until four with Mary; then Shannon and Mama are going to come by. What have you discovered?"

We moved away from the group and briefly filled him in

on what we'd found out. I told him we had more people to talk to in the morning.

"I wish I could help," he said.

"No need. You worry about your dad."

"You could use some sleep," Scott said. "Hiram can take you out to the house. It's on the way to his place."

Hiram did not eagerly say he'd be glad to, but he made no objection. Violet offered, but she lived in town and Scott said it would be silly for her to drive all the way out. I wasn't eager to be alone with Hiram, but I thought this might be a good time to talk to him about the sheriff.

Scott walked with us down to the hospital door and gave me a brief hug. Hiram looked annoyed, but Violet looked pleased.

Hiram led me to a green pickup. In the dim light I could count at least three major dents in the passenger-side door before I got in.

He started the engine, turned the radio up loud, put the car in gear, and jolted out of the parking lot. The noise from the truck told even my untutored ears that he needed a new muffler, or perhaps he'd taken it off. That and the radio noise and we were the loudest thing going down the streets of Brinard. Bumps and potholes didn't seem to bother Hiram. He neither swerved nor slowed for them, with the result that numerous times, we bounced severely about. Twice I hit my head on the cab roof. I guessed this amused him when I saw the side of his mouth rise half an inch both times my head thunked on the roof. I'd looked for seat belts when I first got in, and the truck was new enough to have come with them installed. I didn't see any. He must have taken them out. The truck didn't have air-conditioning, or if it did, Hiram wasn't about to turn it on, and I wasn't about to ask. I matched him by rolling down my window and sticking my elbow out. He gripped the steering wheel with two fingers. I pressed my left hand flat on the seat beside me and held on to the wing-window with my right.

As we passed the edge of town I shouted over the noise, "I'd like to understand why you hate me so much."

He glared at me, then reached over and snapped off the radio. The roar of the mufflerless truck seemed to be swallowed up in the surrounding forest. He said, "Enough to want to take you right now out into Thomas Jefferson Swamp, shoot out one of your kneecaps, and see if you ever come out alive."

Hiram was the biggest of all the Carpenter kids—at least six-six and beefy, but I doubted if much or any of it was fat. His hair was the same color as Scott's, but Hiram's was brush-cut.

"Why not just kill me?"

He stared ahead as we followed our headlights into the soft Georgia night. The breeze from the window made the humidity almost bearable.

"Thought about it. Not sure where to hide the body."

His lip did not curl in slight amusement. This was a very angry man. I braced myself for a possible attack. All I said was, "You must have met gay people before."

"Never."

"What about Scott?"

He glared at me again. Several minutes later we rounded a sharp curve that thrust me against the car door. In the middle of the curve, Hiram said, "Scott is not gay."

This time when he glared at me, he caught me with my mouth open in astonishment. Hiram made a fist and punched the rim of the steering wheel. "He is not gay! He'd never choose to be that way!"

Was there a point in giving him the "We don't choose this" lecture? I tried. "Hiram, as you were growing up, you didn't make a choice. I bet from the earliest you can remember, your sexual thoughts were about girls." He

91

stared straight ahead at the road and gave no indication he heard, but I continued. "When Scott was little, he didn't choose to have sexual thoughts about boys. It was the same for him as it was for you. You had fantasies about girls. He had fantasies about boys. As both of you got older, you wanted women and he wanted men. That's all. It wasn't some goddamn choice."

All Hiram said was, "Scott is not gay."

I thought of graphically describing the things Scott and I did in bed together, but realized anything even slightly detailed might just make him angrier.

"If he says he's gay, why hate me?"

"He's not gay."

I let several miles of silence pass and then said, "I heard you got in a big fight with the sheriff."

"I ain't talkin' to you." With that he flipped the country music station to very loud, straining my budding tolerance for the art form. Not another word did he say until we got to the Carpenter home. He pulled into the end of the drive-way and stopped the car.

I got out, slammed the door, and began to walk the fifty-foot drive to the house in the glow of his headlights. I heard the gears shift and the engine roar. I turned back to look, but the lights of the truck were too bright. For a second it seemed they were coming for me. I flinched toward the underbrush but caught myself. I forced myself to walk calmly down the center of the path. At the same time I waited for the sound of the engine closing in. Pride was one thing, standing there and getting creamed another. Gradually, I heard the truck swing back onto the highway. In seconds the noise was gone and I was in the middle of Georgia darkness. Ahead, through the trees, I thought I could see light from the house.

The moon and the stars gave plenty of illumination as I strode through the otherwise dark night. The humidity was cloying but less than horribly unpleasant. I tried to picture Scott as a kid running through nights just like this. He wouldn't be afraid of the surrounding emptiness. I heard crickets, and frogs, and an owl or two, plus other things I couldn't identify. I thought I might have been half-way to the house when the bushes on my left swayed slightly and I heard unfamiliar rustling. None of the other foliage moved. There was no wind. The movement had to come from something that breathed air. When I stopped, the foliage held still. I walked a few more steps and the movement and noise came again. I strode purposefully forward. I figured it couldn't be a lynch mob, or if it was, they were remarkably quiet for such a large group of people. I wondered if it was a bear. I realized that I didn't know if the state of Georgia had bears, mountain lions, swamp lions—if there were such things—or cougars or lions and tigers. Doubted these last two. The idea of alligators and crocodiles crossed my mind, but I thought, They only live in the Florida Everglades, isn't it, or maybe the bayous of Louisiana? But then I didn't know for sure, and I wasn't eager to wrestle anything that was out in these woods. I hurried my pace, but I refused to run.

◤ 6 ◥

I arrived unlynched at the clearing in front of the house. I opened the door and found Scott's mom and Shannon doing dishes in the kitchen. Mrs. Carpenter heard me, turned, grabbed a dish towel, wiped her hands, and came toward me, smiling shyly. "I'm glad you came with Scott. Can I get you something? Make you a sandwich? Get you a drink of lemonade?"

She was maybe five feet four, with gray hair that saw a beauty parlor at least once a week. She had on a dark brown housedress, the style Edith Bunker always wore. Deep wrinkles grooved her face from nostrils to chin. She would have looked formidable frowning, but she always seemed to be trying to smile.

Shannon had yet to turn and face me. She kept wiping dishes and putting them away in appropriate cabinets. Mrs. Carpenter didn't seem to notice. She said, "I need to bring my husband a few personal things. If you want anything, let me know. Scott showed you everything when he brought you here earlier?"

"Yes, Mrs. Carpenter."

"I ask because you can't be sure with kids, no matter how old they get. They do seem to forget some of the most basic things. You have fresh towels?"

"Yes, ma'am."

"If you'll excuse me . . . I'm afraid my children are right. I'm going to have to get some rest." She leaned heavily on a dining-room chair for a moment.

I moved closer to her and held out my hand. "Can I help?" I asked.

She shook her head, seemed to stretch every muscle, then nodded. "I'm old," she said. She left the kitchen and disappeared through a door on the far side of the living room.

I turned back to Shannon, who was now looking at me. She slapped a plate onto the dish drainer. It cracked in half.

She was about five-nine, with a slender, muscular frame and blond hair slightly darker than Scott's. He had told me she'd been a runner in college. Her body had athletic grace. She wore baggy sweat pants and a shapeless top. She faced me and spoke in a whisper. "You dare stay in this house? You dare defile my parents' home?"

I stepped back. I said, "Everybody keeps telling me that people in the South will never confront you directly. That they'll say things behind your back, but they'd never insult you to your face. They'd never be that rude. I must have missed something. Maybe I'm in the wrong South."

"Rude! I was born in this house. Every one of us has good memories, wholesome memories, of growing up here."

"Your mother invited me."

"She doesn't dare defy Scott. He's the oldest boy, so he gets special treatment. If we had our way, you wouldn't be here."

" 'We' who?"

"Hiram, Nathan, and me."

"But not Mary."

"Ha! Mary's so sweet. Just like Scott—she likes everybody. But she's not here to protect you."

"I wasn't aware I needed protecting. Is this some kind of threat?"

"I hope you get arrested for killing the sheriff. If I could find a way, I'd help implicate you so you'd get thrown in jail. Then we'd get Scott back."

"Why is it so difficult for so many in this family to accept the fact that Scott is gay, that he is very happy and has a good life?"

"Yes, he has a good life. He's rich, and you just live off him."

This was a delicate subject between Scott and me. He was not famous when we met, and, in fact, avoided telling me what he did for three months. At first he said he was a part-time manager of an exercise club, which was accurate. The imminent arrival of the baseball season was the impetus for him to tell me the truth. I think he feared I'd call the media and announce our relationship. No matter how open they are now or claim to have been, every gay person has been in some kind of closet. It might be anything from a slight hesitation about telling a new acquaintance that they're gay to attempting to keep their orientation totally hidden. So even though I didn't like it, I understood. Of course, now he'd called the media himself.

As to the issue of money: Over the years, I'd done numerous things to keep my independence. Many times he'd told me I could quit my job as a teacher, but I never did. I enjoy it too much, and I would never want to live off him. I rebuilt my house a while back after it burned to the ground, but I used the insurance money and my own savings. Yes, he gives me presents that are extravagant beyond my wildest imaginings as a kid, and yes, living in his penthouse on top of a building along Lake Shore Drive in Chicago is fabulous, but I didn't fall in love with him for his money, nor do I stay with him for it. I love him.

I said, "You and the rest of your family have benefited from his wealth directly and indirectly. From his fame, for sure. It must have been incredible growing up as his sister."

"He may have been famous, but I carved my own niche as an athlete. I won some state championships, too. Of course, it was only girl stuff, so I didn't get the recognition. It was always Scott, Scott, Scott. And my hero brother turns out to be a pervert, and he brings that sin into this house."

I wasn't used to fighting with in-laws. My first big tiff had been an hour or so before with Hiram, who did little more than growl at me. Shannon at least spoke to me. I wasn't sure if this was better or not.

"Can we sit down?" I said. "Please."

She remained standing with the dish towel pulled taut between her fists. "Just say what you have to say."

"Look," I said. "I don't expect cheers and parades, and I'm sorry you don't like me, but I love your brother more than anything else on this earth. I would do anything for him. Make any sacrifice for him. He is more precious than anything in the world to me. I'll help him through this time with his father, and he and I will leave. I wish I was more welcome, but that doesn't seem possible. If we can't begin trying to be friends, can we at least agree to be civil while I'm here to help Scott?"

Her eyes were those of a zealot in the face of the infidel. She turned her back on me. I gave up. I had more problems than whether my in-laws liked me or not.

Upstairs, I brushed my teeth, took off everything but my underwear, and crawled between the sheets.

I tossed and turned for some time while the glow of the full moon entered through a window facing east. I fell asleep wondering if you could see motes of dust in moon-light streaming through a window the same way you could in sunbeams.

When I awoke, it was daylight. Scott lay on top of the other bed. He was in his briefs and lying on his stomach. I stared at the white ceiling, afraid to move much for fear of waking him, although he usually slept very soundly. I hadn't heard him come in, which testified to my own state of exhaustion. Nature's needs eventually caused me to slip on some jeans and hurry to the bathroom. I reentered the room and closed the door softly.

"It's okay, I'm awake," he said. He turned over on his side and propped his chin on his hand.

I sat on the side of his bed.

"How's your dad?"

"Slept peacefully through the night. Mama and Shannon are there. I got here about six. What time is it?"

I looked at my watch. "Nearly ten."

He eased his head back down. "I'd like to sleep for a week."

I patted his arm. "How's your muscle strain?"

"Practically haven't noticed it." He grinned. "You might want to massage it now."

I looked around the room. "Here? Now?"

"Very definitely now."

I glanced at the front of his shorts. "Looks like you're in the mood for more than a massage."

"I know it's goofy, but sitting with my dad, I'd think about a lot of past stuff, but I'd also think about holding you and being with you and doing stuff with you, and . . ." He blushed.

"And what?"

"I've always wanted to make it with a guy in my own bed in my old room at home."

"This does seem to be that venue. What if somebody's in the house and hears us?"

"I told you, they left. If Nathan's here, he's outside working."

"He could stop in."

"We'll be quiet. He won't be jealous anyway." He let the fingers of his right hand slowly caress the tips of the fingers on my left hand. He stroked each finger from tip to base, moved to my palm and then slowly onto my wrist.

I remember taking one of my boyfriends in high school back to my house when I knew nobody would be home. We never made it to my room, but had a wild time in the rec room in the basement. Doing it on the couch in my parents' house was one of the hottest sexual moments of my youth.

Most often our lovemaking is slow and sensuous, and this time Scott seemed ready to let each caress take an eternity. I lay back and let his hands rove over my body, and eventually I did the same to him.

When his hand began exploring the front of my pants, I pulled him to me. I swung my legs round, put one arm under his head, my hand on his hip and pulled him close. I held his strong, muscular body tightly. The agonizingly gentle caresses were replaced with mad, passionate kisses and fierce embraces.

A long while later he breathed deeply, his mouth next to my right ear, and whispered, "That was unbelievable."

"I'd be content to lie here like this with you for several centuries." I held him tightly. I felt his breathing slow and his muscles relax. I let my hands gently rove over his back in slow circles. I enjoyed the feel of the weight of his body on mine. I felt warm and safe and protected.

Someone knocked at the door. Scott jumped to his feet.

We both pulled on pants. Scott opened the door. It was Nathan.

"Didn't know if you were here," he said.

"We're here," Scott said. "Any news from the hospital?"

"No." I thought I caught Nathan trying to look further into the room. Was he the sex police, or interested?

"We'll be down in a few minutes," Scott said.

We showered, dressed, and met in the kitchen. We had orange juice. Nathan was nowhere to be seen.

"We can eat in town," Scott said.

"I can fill you in on all the details from yesterday. There wasn't much time at the hospital."

I phoned the library and set up a meeting with Violet for early in the afternoon. After a call to the hospital, we strode out into the humidity.

"All this damp, you'd think it would pour rain," I said.

"Supposed to. Tropical depression that's been developing over the Gulf of Mexico is moving in this afternoon."

"We aren't going to have to evacuate or something like that?"

"A tropical depression is not a hurricane."

"I knew that."

"Mostly in June storms start over the Gulf of Mexico and don't get that strong. Not like hurricanes later on in the summer. We're not that near to the coast, so mostly we just get lots of rain. Farmers could use it."

Out front was a pearl-gray BMW.

"Where'd this come from?"

"Am I fabulously rich?"

"Undoubtedly."

"Therefore phone calls can be made and deliveries can occur, even in Brinard."

"I'm suitably impressed."

Other than what I considered essential for a car—four

wheels and the ability to go—this one also had blessed air-conditioning.

I was curious about Nathan's trying to see into the bedroom, so I asked. "Nathan seemed kind of interested in what we were doing," I said.

"Nah, he's straight."

"Well, you hear about all these incestuous southern-gothic sexual escapades between brothers and brothers, or brothers and sisters, and what all."

"You have got to stop being so prejudiced. I never touched any of my brothers or sisters. They never put a move on me. That's all overblown bull. I watched a few animals screw out in the barn when I was four or five. Wasn't exciting then and I ignored it the rest of the time I was growing up. As for Nathan, I accidentally walked in on him when he was more than making out with a girl in the barn."

"Just thought I'd ask."

"He's got his own place a couple miles down the road. Got a wife and four kids. He kind of runs both farms now and hires help during the busy seasons. Daddy does what he can when he's in the mood."

I told him everything that had happened the night before. Scott was furious at Hiram and Shannon. I thought about not telling him what they'd said, balancing the feeling of tattling with the fact that Scott was an adult. He could deal with the information any way he saw fit. My general policy was that withholding information was childish and stupid.

This noon we chose to dine at the exquisite and well-appointed Huddle House. A bright-eyed and bubbling teenager served us. She seemed quite pleasant and unaffected by the word on us. In the newspaper boxes out front, the death of the sheriff held the headlines. Scott's presence in town was little more than a sports-page squib—mostly speculation about whether he was really in the South for his father's illness or merely in hiding because of the headlines.

Scott was more concerned about family politics than he was about the sports world. "I'll talk to Hiram and Shannon," he said. "They may not like my being gay, but this is bullshit. As for that crap you heard Hiram and Nathan saying the other night . . ." He sighed. "I tried talking to Nathan last night. I think he listened. It's this damn religious stuff down here that makes it so tough. Shannon and Hiram are real religious. Nathan told me Hiram had joined Reverend Hollis's church."

"That's not going to help."

"Plus I think they believe that I've betrayed my family. Somehow, all these headlines reflect on them. Like I chose to be gay."

"Is it worth a family fight at a time like this?" I asked.

He thought a minute. "If there's a good time to say something, I will. I guess it'll depend some on how Daddy's doing. Did that young cop really admit to dancing in Atlanta?"

"Sure did. I wouldn't mind seeing one of his performances. At least it gave us some leverage."

"I don't think that stuff about Hiram and the sheriff was important. Those kinds of fights aren't big deals around these parts."

I kept silent. I wasn't eliminating anybody from my list of possible suspects, no matter what their relationship to Scott.

"You know anything about a guy named Jasper Williams, local eccentric, skinhead, and budding Nazi?"

"Never heard of him. The town eccentric when I was growing up was Theodore Horst. He owned a flower shop on the square. He lisped and swished. I thought that's what it meant to be gay. It was part of the reason it took me so long to come out to myself. I thought I'd have to be like him."

We finished eating and returned to the car. "I'm supposed to meet Violet later," I said. "You can go to the hospital, and I can try and keep from being arrested."

He dropped me off at the library.

Today, Violet wore a bright yellow-and-green flower-print dress. She introduced me to Lisa, the woman taking her place at work.

Lisa shook my hand and said, "I'm happy to meet you. I hope you don't think everyone in this town is in the hands of the preachers and the bigots. There's lots of folks who are sympathetic. Course, they're afraid some, but I know you didn't kill the sheriff. He was a mean man."

"How so?" I asked.

"Us kids used to just hang out in the parking lot of the Piggly Wiggly—that's the grocery store—on Friday and Saturday nights. Used to be we could just be there to talk to our friends, but the last few years he'd come by, not just send a deputy to warn us, and he'd get all ugly. Nobody liked it, but we couldn't complain to our parents. He was just bein' mean."

I sympathized with this dastardly behavior.

"Violet says y'all might talk to Jasper Williams?"

I nodded.

"You be careful. All of us kids grew up scaring each other with stories about him. I know kids do that a lot, try to scare each other, but we all know Jasper is a mean man."

I thanked her for the warning.

Violet grabbed an oversized bag and we left. "Who do you want to talk with first?" she asked. She started the Cadillac and turned on the air-conditioning.

"I'd like to begin with Clara Thorton. She seems to be the

biggest honcho around here, and she had the nerve to stand up to Peter Woodall."

"I thought you might. I called and set up an appointment."

We drove directly to the courthouse. Outside, a few people sat on cement benches in the shade. Inside, the floors were highly polished wood. The walls were painted beige, with black-and-white photos of the early days of the courthouse, showing mules, horses, buggies, and people traversing the unpaved street.

Clara Thorton's office was in the front on the second floor. She had a light orange rug, blond chairs, a teak desk, and several filing cabinets. Each wall had two paintings of antebellum homes: Classical and Gothic Revival on one, Federal and Regency on the other.

Clara put on her gold-rim glasses and stood to meet us. She wore a black skirt, a white blouse with a Peter Pan collar, and strands of pearls around her neck. Violet formally introduced us.

Clara's watery gray eyes stared at me uncompromisingly. She said, "I agreed to see you, Mr. Mason, because Violet asked me. I was also intrigued, maybe even pleased, when you held your temper with Peter in the Waffle House. I admire self-control."

"It took a lot," I said.

"Don't mistake me," she said. "I appreciate what you did, but I'm not fond of you or your lifestyle."

"What lifestyle is that?" I asked. "The one where I teach school? The one where I go home and read books? The one where I go to movies, and eat dinner, or laugh or cry or care for someone I love, or the one where I have a mother and father and brothers and sisters who I love and care for as much as they love and care for me?"

Violet said nothing to interrupt me.

Clara said, "You're very bold for someone who is a thin

line away from being arrested for murder."

I spoke very quietly. "I didn't kill anyone. I found the body and now I'm going to find the killer, since the local police don't seem to be interested in doing that."

"Insulting me won't help that," Clara said.

"Treating me like dirt, talking down to me, won't find out who killed the sheriff."

"Depends if I really care who killed the sheriff, and if I really care what happens to you, doesn't it?"

"I appreciate your honesty."

Violet said, "Clara, I know you've had a feud with the sheriff for years. Everybody in the county knows it."

"And you think that makes me a murder suspect?" She smiled for about two seconds and laughed for maybe five.

"It makes you a better suspect than me," I said.

"Maybe I'll talk to Judge Collins, convince him to have you arrested. I don't know what kind of pull your lawyer friend had, but we folks in this county have our ways as well."

"What did you feud with the sheriff about?" Violet asked.

"You know as well as I do, Violet. There are few secrets in this county."

"I know that you didn't like each other," Violet said, "but I haven't really been in town much since I was a kid."

I said, "Mrs. Thorton, I understand you don't like me. I apologize if my words a few minutes ago offended you. I feel cornered and trapped just being in this town, and since I discovered the body I've been pretty uptight. I'd like to do what I can to clear my name. It looks like solving the crime is the only way for that to happen. I'd appreciate any help you can give me."

She picked up a gold pen from the top of her desk and tapped it against the blotter. She took off her glasses and leaned back in her chair. She looked from Violet to me.

She said, "I don't like homosexuals. I hope the preachers can organize and make a concerted statement. I hope we don't have an uproar in this town, but we're starting to get lots of publicity. I've heard rumors of a homosexual-rights activist coming to town, and I've been told the Atlanta papers are sending people here. Some tabloid creature was annoying people this morning in the Waffle House. The connection with the famous Scott Carpenter and a possible murder is a tremendous lure."

She thought for a moment more, then leaned forward in her chair and propped her elbows on the top of the desk. "Being elected county commissioner the past couple elections has not been easy. These men would like to get me out. A big blowup about this case in the press would be bad. But if you didn't do it, and they look stupid because of how they handled it, I'd be able to use it against them."

Abruptly she pulled her chair closer to her desk. She said, "The sheriff liked to collect secrets, and that's how he preferred getting elected. If someone did something, he might or might not arrest him."

"I don't understand," I said.

"Say the bank president's son was arrested for possession of marijuana—a reasonably serious offense in this county and in this state. Maybe the sheriff would go to the bank president and talk to him. Then the kid got off, and next election one of Peter's big supporters would be the bank president."

"This happened?"

"Just an example. You'll have to find the specifics. The only reasonably solid rumor I ever got was that the sheriff had some dirt on Al Holcomb."

"Even I know he's the Klan leader in town," I said.

"So does everybody. That wouldn't be the secret he'd hold over his head. I've always kind of wanted to know what the secret is. When I first took office, Peter tried to bully me by threatening to reveal things from my husband's past, but I dared him to do his worst. He never did try. Came in the first day I was in office and tried to get me to knuckle under. That's why I've always hated him. How dare he!"

"What did he have on your husband?" I asked.

"None of your business."

We all paused at this barrier for a second.

I asked, "Who else in town had a grudge against him?"

"Everybody tiptoed delicately around the sheriff. You might try Wainwright Richardson, county coroner and your immediate nemesis. There's a feud there that goes way back. I know their families openly quarreled for a while in the late forties. Don't know about what. My husband probably knew, but he didn't pass any political information on to me. I've had to win elections without threatening everybody—I've just had to do a good job."

"Did the sheriff get along with his wife?" I asked.

"Haven't heard about any problems. She's stayed home to raise the kids. Had one almost nine months to the day after they got married."

In the hallway after the interview I said, "I'm sorry about getting annoyed with her and letting it show, but I'm tired of being the stepped-on pansy in this town."

"They aren't used to an uppity queer," Violet said. "They'll survive. Richardson's office is downstairs—let's try him before we leave."

His room was not as large, but in most other respects it was identical to Clara's, except his pictures were of battleships, aircraft carriers, and submarines.

Richardson wore a charcoal-gray suit and smoked a pipe. He did not ask our permission if he could light up. He pulled a pouch out of his top left drawer, inserted the tobacco into his pipe, tamped it down, lit it, and blew smoke rings in our direction. It actually smelled pretty good, sort of a cherry flavor.

"Working on getting you arrested," he said.

"Working on finding out who really killed him," I said.

Violet said, "Wainwright, we need help."

He turned to her. "I don't see why you're helping him, Violet. It's all around town about you driving up here with him this afternoon. Somebody thought they might have seen you two together last night."

"Wainwright," she asked, "aren't you interested in finding out who killed the sheriff?"

"I don't want both of these jobs," Wainwright said. "I'd prefer to be coroner of Brinard County. I'm not interested in this sheriff business, and I don't want to investigate. Want to just get done with my job and get in as much fishing as I can."

"You're going to convict me because you're too lazy?"

"You don't like honesty?"

"What did your family quarrel about with the sheriff's?" Violet asked.

"Who told you that?"

"Clara."

"Should have kept her mouth shut."

None of us spoke as Wainwright puffed on his pipe for several moments. Finally he said, "That quarrel can't have anything to do with why the sheriff died."

"What was it?" Violet asked.

"Peter's daddy and I served in the same outfit in World War II, and we saw action together in Africa and Italy. He accused me of being a coward in the war and tried to get people here to believe it. His daddy was an ignorant blowhard, but some people will believe anything. I never had a quarrel with Peter, but his daddy was unforgiving. I suppose it didn't help that I bought as much land around his property as I could. When Peter inherited his land, I tried to buy it from him. He never was much of a farmer. Practically drove himself and all his kin to bankruptcy. He may have had reason to kill me, but I had no reason to kill him. My family started with more money, and I made the family richer. Peter was almost broke when he became sheriff. He got elected because he was a sports hero in high school. Course, it could have been worse. What if Scott Carpenter had stayed in town? He was such a hero, he could have gotten himself elected anything—and look where we'd be. A homosexual sheriff."

"Is the autopsy report on the sheriff in yet?" I asked.

"I've gotten some reports."

"It would help if I could get some details about his death. Was he drugged? Did he struggle? Where was he?"

Wainwright laughed. "Why would I have to give my prime suspect that information? You should know it already. I can tell you one little thing. We found plenty of your fingerprints at the scene. We're going to take your buddy's so we can eliminate his."

"You'll find everybody's prints who's rented the car or who worked at the car rental agency. Prints don't mean anything."

"I'm going back to Judge Collins with the state's attorney again today. Maybe this time we'll get a warrant. I was surprised when you pulled that much power out of a hat. I thought we had you."

He would tell us no more, and moments later he stood up and led us out of the room.

His secretary said, "Mr. Wainwright, there are reporters outside the door, three or four of them. One is from the *Truth Express,* that horrible gossip paper."

"Can you let us out a quieter way?" Violet asked.

Richardson puffed on his pipe once or twice and then grinned. "They'll find you. This town isn't that big, but sure." He opened a side door and ushered us into a narrow hallway and then into a vacant courtroom. He pointed to a door on the opposite wall. "That way." He turned and left.

Outside the door was a man in his mid-twenties. He wore faded blue jeans, a blue-and-white striped shirt, and a brightly colored tie. He was five-nine and maybe all of one hundred thirty pounds. His most striking facial feature was a sea of prominent zits.

"I knew I picked the right door," he said. "I knew you wouldn't want to come out the front way. Those national reporters aren't so goddamn smart. Yes!" He jerked his left arm in the annoying pumping gesture of triumph currently popular. Light from fluorescent tubes overhead glinted off his silver wire-rimmed glasses. "I'm from the *Burr County Clarion*," he continued.

"Aren't you Dennis?" Violet asked. "Mrs. Hale's boy? I thought you were at college."

"I graduated last year. I've been working for the paper. They've got everybody trying to dig up stuff about Scott Carpenter's past, talking to everybody who knew him." He pointed to me. "Nobody seems to care a lot about you, except as a murder suspect."

We stood in a back entrance of the courthouse and watched enormous black clouds drifting toward us from the southeast.

"Don't they care who killed the sheriff?" I asked.

"Everybody thinks you did it. The regular courthouse reporter on the paper just calls Wainwright Richardson or goes over to the police station and talks to all his buddies."

"But you don't have any contacts," I said.

"No, sir. Plus I don't think you did it."

"Thank you."

"I want to help, and, to be honest, if I get the real story, it'll be a big boost to my career. It could make the wire services, and I could get out of this town."

"You could leave now," I said. "Got to be some jobs in bigger towns for kids just out of journalism school."

"Not many at all. I tried for six months. For the last two weeks in Nashville, I only had enough money to buy eggs and day-old bread."

"I appreciate your offer of help," I said. I didn't know if he could be trusted, and I figured I was going far enough relying on Violet.

"I know you don't have a reason to trust me, and I'm not going to say that some of my best friends are gay, although there were gay guys at the university. Some were okay, some not, like everybody else. I've got a girlfriend, so I'm not some closet case. I just think you've gotten a raw deal, and maybe I can hitch my career to the truth. I wouldn't mind that. Make some of these people realize what a good reporter they lost."

"What do you think, Violet?" I asked.

"It's not like you've got so many friends in town that you can afford to be picky." She smiled at Dennis. "You might not remember, but I do, Dennis. I used to baby-sit for you when you were little. You used to always bring books and more books for me to read to you. You asked me once what these were." She pointed to her breasts. "Then you tried to grab one. You were precious at five."

Dennis blushed. "Did I really?"

"I held your little hand carefully that night." She laughed. "We need all the help we can get."

"What's the plan?" Dennis asked.

"First of all, we're trying to find out the results of any of the police tests."

He shook his head. "I can't help you there. The cops would never tell me any secrets. If Jackson—he's the courthouse reporter—has information, he'll never give it to me. I'm just a twerp to him. He just tells me to shut up, do the obits, and attend the meetings that he thinks are boring."

"We might have a contact on that," Violet said. She didn't name Cody or how we could get the information. Dennis might be on our side, but why test his gentle loyalty with one of our best pieces of leverage?

"Who else have you talked to besides Clara and Wainwright?"

I gave him a look.

"Well, it's not a big secret. Everybody saw you walk in. Wasn't hard to find out where you've been."

"What we need to know are people who didn't like the sheriff or people he had secrets on, who might have been scared of him. Somebody with a motive to kill him."

"I don't know," Dennis said. "I'm pretty young to know that kind of stuff, and I've been away at college. Nobody at the paper would confide that kind of stuff to me. Although Dr. McLarty stopped me this morning and wanted to know what I knew about the murder. He also asked if I'd talked to you, and if I knew where you were staying."

"That's Scott's dad's doctor," I said. "You think he knows something?"

"We should at least talk to him," Violet said.

"I'd also like to talk to this Jasper Williams," I said. "If he's the local Nazi, he might be capable of anything. Supposedly, he's harmless, but we heard a story about some hikers that showed him capable of violence. Jasper is high on my suspect list."

"He *is* crazy," Dennis said.

"That's what Lisa indicated at the library."

"I'm not sure where exactly he lives," Violet said. "Certainly not so that I could drive you there—plus I wouldn't want to go. It's someplace in Thomas Jefferson Swamp, and it's supposed to be really strange."

112

"It's not just a rumor," Dennis said. "I've been there, once."

"Why on earth for?" Violet asked.

"It was a big joke at the paper. They do it to all the new kids, send them out to talk to Jasper. It was sure strange out there. He was in my class at school. Everybody avoided him. He dropped out in ninth grade and nobody missed him."

"Did he used to torture animals and set fires?" I asked.

"No. . . . Why? Should he?"

"Classic patterns of a serial killer," I said.

"I don't know about that. He was just weird. Talked to himself. He slapped a teacher in first grade. Bit a girl in third grade. Mostly he kept very quiet. He never raised his hand and sat by himself at lunch. During all of sixth grade, whenever he walked anywhere, he would goosestep. Fat little nerdy kid all those years."

"What happened when you went out there?"

"It was freaky. I left in a hurry."

"Why?"

He hesitated, then shrugged. "I never actually saw him. It just . . . well, I just heard this whispery voice telling me to go. So I went."

He seemed uninclined to elaborate. I wondered how frightened he'd been. Telling the story with an elaborate amount of detail might damage his code of masculinity.

"We have anybody else in town to talk to?" I asked.

Violet said, "While you're out trying to talk to Jasper, I can try and see Leota. I don't think it's a good idea for you to go with me to see her, you being a suspect and all."

I agreed.

"Plus," Violet continued, "I can try and find out some of that police-report material. Be careful out there. Don't turn your back on him." She gazed at the darkening horizon to our south and east. "If it starts to rain hard, get out of the swamp."

"We had a dry spring, and it hasn't rained but a quarter of an inch for six weeks," Dennis said. "It could rain a foot and it wouldn't raise the level of the swamp much."

"Just be careful," Violet warned. She got in her Cadillac while Dennis and I walked to the other side of the square and got into his Volkswagen Beetle. It was painted a dull brown and did not have air-conditioning. He shifted gears and pulled out.

"You know it's not going to be a secret you're helping me," I said. "Half the town must have seen us talking together."

"I don't care if they think I'm gay. I know I'm not."

"You don't think it'll hurt your career if you're seen with the number-one murder suspect in the history of the county?"

"I'm not going to be hanging around this burg that long. And you're not the biggest killer ever in these parts."

"Who has that honor?"

"Billy Joe Barnett back in the 1890s did in most of his kin one hot summer night. Biggest flood ever in the county. It had stopped raining, but the waters were still rising. Thought he could get away with it by drowning them all in the rush of water. Rescue workers came by in time to see him holding his aunt Jessie's head underwater."

We drove out the same road that led to Scott's house, but instead of turning at the first left past the second crumbling gas station we continued straight for at least another fifteen miles.

"How'd you find your way the first time?" I asked.

"They've got a mimeographed set of directions at the paper that they drag out."

"And you remember the way?"

"As long as you get the first turn correct, you can't miss

it. Once you're off this road you take every fork or possible turn to the right."

He slowed down when we got about a mile past a little red schoolhouse that looked like it came right out of a first-grade primer.

Dennis said, "This is the tough part." A car behind us honked and then sped past. On our left giant weeping willow trees bent their branches all the way to the road. The more violent gusts of a rising wind whipped the branches nearly horizontal. A few fat raindrops spattered down on the car, then stopped. Going slowly caused the breeze from the windows to die, and between gusts of wind the car was nearly unbearable.

"Hell of a lot of humidity in the air," I said.

" 'Bout the same as usual. Still, we could get a mess a rain." His eyes inspected the left side of the road carefully. "There it is." He pulled through what looked to be little more than a gap between two trees.

"Are you sure?" I asked as the car bucked and rocked over what even the most generous person might call an ill-used cattle path. Tree branches and leaves pushed against the car.

"This is right," Dennis said. "I remember it clearly."

"Any particular leaf that looks familiar or just all of them?"

Trees hemmed in the car on both sides and above. The darkening gloom of the afternoon combined with the shadows of the trees made this a twilight world I wasn't happy to be entering. Maybe it would be a good idea to invite Jasper to tea at high noon with half the National Guard in attendance instead of trying this mad trail.

Moments later the car stopped bouncing as much and the trees thinned a little.

"Great," Dennis said. "This is perfect. We've only got a few miles to go."

I was suspicious of his enthusiasm.

"Maybe we should turn back," I suggested.

"Will if you want to, but I thought you needed to talk to this guy."

A path forked to the right and Dennis slowly turned onto it. For a few minutes, my paranoia fought with my need to find the killer. It was daylight and I wasn't alone. "I guess we'll keep going," I said.

Two right turns later, the wind died down and it began to rain. No thunder and lightning, and it wasn't a downpour, just a steady afternoon shower. You'd think with only right turns we'd simply arrive back where we started, but because the serpentine path we followed angled and twisted numerous times, it didn't seem to matter that at every fork or junction we took the way to the right. The rain drummed on the car roof and the engine snarled and whined in that way the old Volkswagen Beetles have, as if the engine were twice as large as it really is.

"Snakes in here?" I asked.

"Yeah."

"Deadly ones?"

"Yeah."

"I don't want to hear about it."

"Okay. As long as you're here, can I ask, what is it like living with Scott Carpenter and being gay and all this coming-out stuff?"

"When all this is over, if we need a reporter, we'll call you. Right now I'd rather concentrate on catching a killer."

"Can't blame me for trying."

I lost count of the number of turns we made. The first rumble of far-off thunder came about ten seconds after Dennis stopped the car.

"Why are we stopping?" I asked.

He pointed to the left. "See that barrel stave around the base of the tree? That's his marker. It's the only left we take. We drive a couple hundred feet to the end of a lane. Then we have to walk about a hundred feet beyond that to get to his place."

"We're going to walk in the rain, aren't we?"

"Unless you know a way of running between the drops."

We turned onto the lane and drove for less than a minute. The thunder and lightning were still distant and infrequent as we got out of the car. As we took our first steps, the rain increased. My head and shirt were soaked in seconds.

"This is nuts," I said. We followed a muddy path, the only sign that humans might be present. About one hundred feet in, as Dennis had said, we came to a clearing about fifty feet wide. On the other side was a small cabin.

Between us and it was an enormous cross, with a six-foot crosspiece and a ten-foot pole embedded in the ground. It was obvious that it had recently been set on fire. Water dripped off a small animal skull that had been nailed to the top of the cross with a large metal spike.

I shuddered and looked beyond it to the cabin. The one window I could see had a lace curtain. An aluminum screen door hung in the entrance. It gleamed as if it had been polished. The front of the cabin was maybe fifteen feet wide. The tips of nails shone on the porch, holding down what looked like newly sawed and regularly spaced pieces of wood. The entire structure was set up on pilings about a foot above the ground.

"You sure he lives here?"

"He has for years."

I pointed to the space under the cabin. "It flood much here?"

He shrugged. "Protects against snakes too."

We crossed the clearing and stepped onto the porch. It seemed sturdy and well made. It was a delight to be out of the rain. Drops covered Dennis's glasses. He pulled out his shirttail to try and dry them. I knocked on the screen door. There didn't seem to be an inner door.

No one answered my knock. I peered through the screen. The cabin seemed to consist of one large room. To the right was a cot, the corners of which were tucked in with military precision. A row of cupboards stretched halfway around the far wall. Below them was a stainless steel sink, a small white refrigerator, and a Franklin stove.

I knocked again. "Nobody home," I said.

Then I heard the *ka-chunk* of a shotgun being pumped.

7

"Don't turn around. Don't move. Don't think. Just obey." A male voice, barely above a whisper.

Dennis began to turn around. Out of the corner of my eye I saw the tip of a shotgun barrel poke its way into the young reporter's ear. Dennis stopped turning and faced front.

"Hands on top of your heads."

I complied. Dennis hesitated. Seconds later he pitched forward. His arms weren't quick enough to break his fall and he slammed face-first into the log wall. Blood spurted from his nose.

"Now you've got it dirty," whispered the voice.

Dennis whimpered.

The butt of the gun smashed down on the back of Dennis's knee. He screamed in agony. I turned to help or fight or escape but got the barrel of the shotgun rammed under my chin.

What startled me into inaction, besides the whap from the shotgun and a gleaming revolver in Jasper's other hand, was my first look at our captor. I was expecting a snaggletoothed behemoth in bib overalls.

What I saw was perhaps the most handsome man I had ever seen. *GQ* would rush to put his face on the cover and

119

thousand-dollar suits on his body. His hair was slightly longer than a brush cut and parted neatly to the side. It gleamed with the rain. His eyes were brown and were shaded by beautiful long lashes—bedroom eyes. His jaw was firm, and the bottom half of his face had the kind of five o'clock shadow that some male models worked to achieve. He was just short of six feet tall, with broad shoulders and narrow hips. He wore a white T-shirt that was damp from the rain, and the fabric clung to his washboard-rippled stomach. He had on black nylon running shorts, cut up each thigh almost to the waistband, with white ankle-length sport socks and black running shoes. Put him in a commercial, and people would stampede to the stores to buy whatever he was selling. The fat little nerd Dennis remembered had long since been transformed.

He never spoke above a whisper.

He said, "Very slowly turn back around. The slightest swift movement and I will kill both of you."

I turned slowly and faced the door.

My hands were seized and a pair of handcuffs applied. Must have taken five seconds, if that much.

"Open the screen door and walk in." He nudged me in the back with the shotgun. Awkwardly, I turned sideways and grabbed the knob. I swung it open as far as I could and then caught it with my elbow. I stepped into the doorway. The rest of the cabin was as pristinely neat as the part I had seen from the porch. He prodded me in the back until I was halfway to the west wall of the cabin. "On the floor," he ordered.

I lay down.

"Turn your head away from the door. If you move it this way, I will kill both of you."

I complied. The corner of the cabin I stared into had one of those all-in-one exercise machines. Like everything else in the cabin, it gleamed as if it had been polished five minutes before. Behind it hung a Nazi flag. To the left of the flag was a five-foot-long aquarium. I thought it odd that it was devoid of water. I saw small mounds of sand with small logs on them. Then one of the logs moved. Snakes. I shut my eyes, and when I opened them I tried to avoid looking looking in the direction of the flag or the creatures.

I heard Jasper put his guns down. Several swift steps followed, and seconds later I felt sure hands grip my ankles. I kicked violently and by luck caught him in the nuts. It took me extra time to get to my feet because my hands were tied, and those few seconds were too many. Something hard crashed into the back of my head. I fell back and smacked my head on the floor. I felt woozy and dizzy. He tied my ankles with leather thongs.

"Don't do that again," he said. "Your death will be ever so much more unpleasant because of it, but remember, I could make it even worse."

I watched him walk to the flag, stepping over the handgun on the floor, and lean the shotgun against the wall. He opened a drawer in the table on which the aquarium sat and pulled out a four-foot-long set of tongs. Then he dragged out what looked like a cane with a loop on the end.

He opened the glass lid of the snake pit, slipped the tongs in, and grabbed one of the vipers just behind the back of the head. He held the squirming beast at arm's length.

Jasper said, "Time for a walk, Bob."

I guess if you live in the middle of a ghastly swamp in Georgia and have guests in to torture, you might as well name your snake something, Bob being as good as any other moniker. I certainly was in no position to tell him it sounded supremely weird.

Bob coiled and writhed. He opened his mouth wide, and I saw acres of white, which framed vicious-looking fangs.

Jasper looped the rope-thing at the end of the cane just behind where Bob's ears would have been, had he had ears. Then, holding the four-foot squirmer at arm's length, Jasper took Bob and set him down so his head was a foot from my nose. Jasper took a metal pin out of the floor, inserted it through a hole in the far end of the cane, let it fall back into the hole in the floor, gave the end of the pin a twist, and stood up.

Bob could now move his head up to about six inches from my face and a foot or so to either side.

"In case you decide to hinder me, Bob will intervene. You've probably never been bitten by a cottonmouth before. It's not pleasant."

There are times in our lives—not many, it's true—when a mad, blind panic seems like the only sensible option. Certainly this was well on its way to being one of those times. I couldn't remember ever being this frightened. I breathed slowly and deeply, tried concentrating on any small opening that could give me an edge in fighting back. There didn't seem to be a lot of those at the moment.

Jasper opened a cabinet and took out a scrub brush, cleaning fluid, and a sponge. I heard the screen door open and close. I guessed he was cleaning up Dennis's blood from the cabin's logs. He reentered, returned to the sink, cleaned the sponge, and replaced everything neatly where it belonged. I saw him pick up the guns, then heard his footsteps. The door swung open but did not close. I heard the click of handcuffs. Finally Jasper said, "Into the cabin."

"I can't move," Dennis said.

"Then I will kill you here." I heard a hammer pulled back. Must have been the handgun he held.

"Okay, okay, okay, okay." Dennis sounded like he was crying. The subsequent whimpering and moaning I heard I took to mean Dennis had begun to move.

"No noises," Jasper commanded.

For the next half-hour I heard the shuffle of a human being dragging himself across the floor. I heard rain pouring on the cabin roof, and saw Bob twisting and squirming at the end of his tether. Dennis couldn't muffle all of his moans and sobs, but Jasper seemed content with the low decibel level of his captive's agony. I didn't hear Jasper's footsteps, so I assumed he stood and watched, certainly made no move to help his victim.

The shuffle-shuffle noise stopped and Dennis said, "I can't."

Footsteps crossed the floor and then Jasper reentered my field of vision. He placed his guns on hooks, turned, and from the wall opposite the aquarium picked up a table. He carried it to the center of the room. He quickly returned to the hooks and picked up his guns. He looked down at me and said, "Shift your body ninety degrees and look in this direction."

I did as commanded. Bob remained between Jasper and me. I prayed for the little thong to hold Bob tightly. I now had a clear view of Jasper's actions.

Dennis lay next to the table. Jasper placed the guns on the table. With one hand he grabbed Dennis by the belt and hefted him onto the table. It wasn't a perfectly smooth move, but he executed the maneuver with incredible ease. From the knees down, Dennis's legs hung past one end of the table. His head rested on the far edge.

Tears, blood, and snot ran down Dennis's face.

Jasper took a rocking chair from a corner and sat down on it, forming a triangle among the three of us. Bob was directly between Jasper and me. The rocker looked as if it had been carved from one piece of wood. It was all white and unvarnished.

"I don't like guests," Jasper said. "You've been here before, Dennis. What did I say last time?"

Dennis sobbed while Jasper rocked.

"What did I say?" Jasper repeated.

"That you'd kill me if I ever came here again."

"Did I ever break a promise I made in school?"

"Jasper," I said. "It's not his fault. He drove me out here because I asked him to. We don't mean to intrude."

"Yes, you did mean to intrude. You came because the sheriff is dead and you're trying to find someone who would be a better suspect than yourself. I'm one of the usual suspects they try to round up when anything goes wrong in this county. Only reason I'm not in jail is because they're afraid to come into my swamp. Doesn't hurt that my daddy owns half the county."

He got up and walked to a cupboard and took out a slim box about eighteen inches wide and twenty-four inches long. He set it down on the floor in front of me so that I could see what he did. It comforted me to know that even Jasper took care not to get in range of Bob's fangs.

He opened the box. It was filled with knives of various sizes. He examined them carefully, then picked out a slender one from the blue-velvet-lined interior. He snapped the lid shut and carefully replaced the box on the floor on the far side of Bob's leash.

Jasper stood next to Dennis's head. "I've been curious about the sheriff's killing," he said. "Lots of secrets in this county, and I know most of them. Usually, I stay in my swamp, but I sneak out when I have a mind to. I thought it was funny last night how Hiram Carpenter made you walk all the way up the driveway. I almost laughed out loud when I rustled that bush and you almost ran out of your pants to get to the house."

"You were there?"

"You know what I've always wanted to do?" he said, then answered his own question. "I've always wanted to play connect-the-dots on somebody's face."

The threat was awful, but I think his constantly talking

in a whisper was the most unnerving thing of all.

Jasper continued, "You know, like connect the dots from zit to zit."

"That's not necessary," I said.

Jasper walked into the kitchen area, opened a drawer, took out a pair of surgeon's gloves, and pulled them on. "Can't be too safe these days, with all these diseases going around. Don't want to infect myself. You never know who might be queer and trying to spread diseases. Always thought you were a fag, Dennis. Even in first grade, I thought you had a bit of a swish."

Dennis's eyes tried to follow what Jasper was doing. I could see the whites around Dennis's gray pupils.

Jasper flipped a knob on a radio. I heard soft country music. Throughout his preparations, Jasper hummed softly along with the music. Songs to torture by. I knew I'd hate the sound of country music as long as I lived, which I hoped would be longer than sunset.

Jasper took several thick towels from a pile in an open cupboard. He folded one several times, then lifted Dennis up by his belt and gently placed the towel under his crotch. He placed the others in a small pile next to his butt. From another drawer he pulled out some rope and tied Dennis's torso to the table. Then he opened the cupboard under the sink and pulled out a plastic dish drainer. He placed a towel under it, and the whole thing under Dennis's head. He returned to the kitchen and came back with numerous smaller towels, three bottles of rubbing alcohol, and a box of cotton balls.

Gently he took Dennis's glasses off and placed them carefully next to the sink.

Dennis tried to wiggle and squirm from his bonds, but Jasper had tied him tighter than a swarm of Eagle Scouts working together for an hour.

Jasper stood with his feet on either side of the table end

near Dennis's head, leaving enough room so that I could see clearly what he was doing.

Jasper said, "You still have zits, Dennis. You should see a dermatologist. But then that won't be a problem after today."

"Leave him alone," I ordered.

Jasper said, "Course now, you're out here investigating. Y'all want to know who would want the sheriff dead." As he talked, Jasper gently lifted Dennis's head as carefully as if he were a diamond cutter choosing where to carve the next facet of a jewel beyond price.

"Lots of people didn't like the sheriff. Especially women who couldn't fight back. He used to take advantage of them a lot. I never put a stop to it, because I enjoyed watching when I could. Instead of arresting young ladies who were in trouble, he'd often as not take them into the backseat of his police car. Bet they could find all kinds of interesting things if they took a microscope to the back of his car. He never saw me watching. Best show in town on a Saturday night. I was going to buy a video camera so I could film it and give him a Christmas present. Died too soon."

He let Dennis's head down gently so that his victim's nose faced in my direction. He entwined his fingers in Dennis's hair and gripped tightly. Jasper said, "The biggest zit is here." He placed the knife next to a yellow-headed pimple in the middle of Dennis's chin. "And the next largest seems to be here." Jasper sliced a bloody furrow from the chin to the side of Dennis's nose. Dennis screamed and tried to yank his head away. He was barely able to move his face a quarter-inch, but the rest of his body twisted and spasmed. The ropes held him to the shaking table. Blood flowed from the four-inch-long gouge in Dennis's face. The skin on either side of the cut flapped open. If Dennis lived, he would be scarred for life.

I went berserk. I began bellowing epithets at Jasper and

coiling myself backwards, attempting to leverage myself for some kind of spring at him.

Jasper grabbed a gun and aimed it at me.

Keeping Bob between us, Jasper edged to the aquarium, took the tongs, opened the glass lid, and plucked out another viper.

"Do you know how a person dies from the bite of a cottonmouth?" he asked. Jasper provided the answer I didn't want to hear. "It dissolves the tissue it comes in contact with, and the swelling spreads out from where a person gets bitten. It itches some, and pretty soon you'll want to scratch a whole whale of a lot. Then you sort of collapse and die. Course, sometimes this doesn't happen all at once. Can take ten minutes or a lot longer. Depends."

He swung the snake in my direction. I became very quiet.

"Over here," he ordered, pointing to the original spot I'd been in.

I moved slowly, my eyes never leaving the thing at the end of Jasper's tongs.

"This is Roy," Jasper said. "I named all the snakes after the therapists I had as a kid. Bob and Roy were the first two counselors, and the first two cottonmouths I caught." Once again he shoved the creature inches from my nose. Then he secured the rope-thing behind its head, placed the end of the cane onto the floor, and pinned it in place. Bob was still between me and the table with Dennis. Roy lurked on the other side of me. The only direction I could move now was backwards, maybe three feet to the aquarium, where more snakes were encaged.

On the table Dennis's body continued to jerk spasmodically. An acrid stench reached my nostrils. I understood why Jasper had placed the towel under Dennis's middle. Then for a while Dennis didn't move. I figured he'd passed out. The towel and drainer mat under his face caught the blood that poured out. Almost lovingly Jasper cleaned Dennis's wound, once going to the sink and pouring water on a washcloth to rinse out the mess created on it. When he finished cleaning, he stood back a few feet to examine his work. He came within six inches of Bob, whose mouth gaped open as he lunged to the end of his tether. Jasper never even looked in the snake's direction. He did not deal with the towel under Dennis's middle.

I tried to think of a way to get free and save us, but nothing seemed likely. Jasper returned to the kitchen area and came back with a small vial. This he placed under Dennis's nose. Eventually Dennis came around. His eyes blinked at me. He began alternately crying, screaming, and begging. "God, it hurts! . . . I'm sorry! . . . Please, let me go! . . . I'm sorry! I'm sorry! . . . Please don't hurt me anymore!"

Jasper sat in his rocking chair and let Dennis babble on like this until the young reporter was hoarse with his pleading.

When Dennis was quiet, Jasper returned to his position six inches in back of Dennis's head.

"No!" Dennis screamed.

He fainted again. Jasper revived him and began the same type of preparations he'd done before the first cut. The preparation again seemed to take an eternity.

Jasper resumed speaking in his chatty whisper, as if his best friends had come to an intimate tea party. "Now, the sheriff was having intercourse with anything female that moved. Maybe an angry husband decided to do him in. Hard to tell." All this while his eyes roved and his hands gently probed the skin on Dennis's face, in a pore-by-pore inspection.

I heard the radio playing softly, occasional thunder, Dennis's whimpers, Jasper's whispering or humming, Bob and Roy rustling, the whine of bugs and mosquitoes, and the continuous thud of rain hitting the roof. I could feel several bugs biting. A few landed on Jasper, but he never brushed them off. If a mosquito landed, it got a meal and then flew off.

"Of course, it could have been Al Holcomb. Old Al thinks the world revolves around his penis and the Ku Klux Klan. I'm the only one besides the sheriff who knows Al has a black mistress deep in Thomas Jefferson woods."

He took the knife and slashed a path between two pimples three inches apart on Dennis's forehead. Dennis screamed and passed out again. Jasper took his bottle of rubbing alcohol and several cotton swabs and cleaned the blood off of Dennis's face. When the bleeding stopped, Jasper took the towel, rinsed it thoroughly, and placed it back under Dennis's face. Jasper cleaned him up, revived him as often as necessary, and then began hunting for a new spot.

He picked up speaking exactly where he had left off, as if inflicting these ghastly wounds were as meaningless as knitting a shawl. "Having a black mistress is not considered good form among fellow Klan members. Still have trouble with interracial couples in this neck of the woods. Course, a black man with a white woman would still cause quite a stir. Sort of like faggots. If they kept quiet, they probably wouldn't be harassed on the street, but late at night, my the things you can do to scare people."

I tested the handcuffs again. My hands weren't going anywhere. I could move my feet a few inches, but my ankles were absolutely not going to part without help from another appendage. I could maneuver my knees some. If the impetus for physical action was going to happen, it would be from them, which seemed kind of pointless. Leaping to one's knees to subdue an unencumbered opponent was on the stupendously stupid end of the spectrum of options.

"Listen, Jasper," I said. "Please let him go. Don't hurt

him anymore. We really mean you no harm. Can't you just listen?" I continued speaking even past the point when I figured he wasn't paying the slightest attention. He simply kept humming and checking Dennis's head. Finally I let out a roar that must have come close to rupturing my vocal cords. "You listen to me, you son-of-a-fucking-bitch." I gasped for air. He simply got up and walked carefully to the other end of Roy's cane/leash. He unhooked the end and moved it so Roy's gaping maw came to within three inches of my face. I shut up.

Jasper started another round of inspecting Dennis's head. By this time the young reporter's eyes were glazed. Jasper had him conscious, but only by a little.

"Now, Hiram Carpenter is a secretive fellow. I wouldn't trust that whole family. My daddy never liked them much. Always so high and mighty with their big-deal faggot son. Hiram's a thief. Always has been. Tried desperately as a kid to outshine his brother, but never could match him. He has this huge spread in the north part of the county. For a while I thought he grew drugs or maybe imported them, but old Hiram's a clever one. I'm not sure what he's up to. I think the sheriff was on to him about something. Course, each one is sneakier than the others. Got too much religion in that crowd. Thought Nathan was going to be a good Nazi for a while, but he chickened out. Got religion at a tent revival one year. Poor sap. Shannon Carpenter is sneaky. She's been up to something lately. I'm not sure what. Quitting her job unexpectedly. Leaving the house in the middle of the night for trysts with somebody. I'll find out who. Has to be illegal."

Jasper placed the knife against a large zit in the middle of Dennis's cheek. "Nothing to connect this to," Jasper said. He inserted the knife and twisted. This time Dennis's body nearly came off the table, which shuddered and moved several inches. If evil swamp creatures truly ex-

130

isted, they would have fled at the sound of Dennis's howl of agony.

Agonizing minutes later, when Jasper got done cleaning and reviving, I could see a half-inch-diameter patch of white in the middle of Dennis's cheek. Jasper had cut through to the bone. It took quite some time for him to stanch the blood enough so that nothing covered the hole he had made.

Finally Jasper stood in front of Dennis again. He'd cleaned and washed out towels after each session; twice emptied the dish drainer of accumulated blood. Before he started, everything had to be neat and in place.

"Now then, you don't know about Preacher Hollis. He does not like you boys. Course, I don't either. The saintly little pudge gets up on Sundays and threatens his fellow sinners with hellfire and damnation. I enjoy his sermons. Try never to miss them. Reminds me of Jonathan Edwards and 'Sinners in the Hands of an Angry God.' I got hold of all of Jonathan's sermons that have survived. Memorized all of them. Bet that's a surprise to you, Dennis. Thought I was stupid in school. Wasn't stupid. Just never cared much for it.

"Well, our sheriff never did get much below the age of consent with his escapades with women, but I'm afraid our preacher has gone far below the legal age to satisfy his carnal desires. If I had a little girl, I wouldn't let her go on a field trip with the preacher."

"*The* Preacher Hollis?" I asked. "The one who did so much to out Scott?" I didn't know whether to believe Jasper or not. If it was true, it gave us a powerful weapon.

Jasper didn't answer me. For a few minutes he chuckled to himself or hummed along with the music. Without warning he resumed: "I've actually got pictures of our holy preacher damaging the goods. Sheriff just found out."

He sighed and looked at me. "You know the problem

with everything I've told you?" He didn't wait for my answer. "Unfortunately, I don't actually know who killed the sheriff. I also have to admit that while I'm good at sneaking around this county and getting information, some of this has come from inside the police department. You just can't trust anybody these days. However, the main problem is, you're both going to be dead, and you're never going to be able to use any of this information."

I noted that Dennis seemed more conscious than he had been in a while. At least his eyes followed the movement of the knife carefully. As Jasper swung it back and drove it toward his face again, Dennis jerked back. The sudden movement caused Jasper to miss his aim, but not for the better. No matter where it was supposed to land, I saw the knife start above and to the left of Dennis's left eye and cut a furrow down and over the eye. Dennis's subsequent scream raised the hair on the back of my head.

The spasms of his body, whether voluntary or involuntary, as it tried to get away from this invasion, launched the table forward. Not far, but enough that it hit Jasper's midsection and caused him to lose his balance and tumble to the floor. Bob struck. I saw his jaws close on Jasper's tanned calf. The guns on the table clattered to the floor on the far side of the table.

Jasper whirled around and in seconds had his hands wrapped around the far end of Bob's tail. Jasper began twirling the snake over his head. He was screaming at the top of his lungs and not paying attention to me. I was glad to hear something more human than the incessant monotone whisper.

I could now move into the area no longer guarded by the snake on my right. I rolled to my side, tucked my legs under me, and leveraged myself to a crouching position. Jasper faced away from me as he swung the snake. I could maneuver my feet maybe three inches at a time. I moved as silently and as quickly as I could. Jasper twirled suddenly and slammed the snake's head down on the tabletop. As best I could, I hurled myself at him. The weight of my body propelled him across the cabin. His back and head crashed into the side of the door. His head banged against a protruding hinge and he lay still.

All this took maybe five seconds.

I thought about the guns, but it wouldn't do much good for me to hold them in my manacled hands behind my back while trying to get myself free.

I turned to Dennis. His head was turned away from me. The snake's body lay on the floor. Its head was completely smashed. I hopped to Dennis and saw his face. The knife had fallen to the floor. The last cut bled profusely. The initial point of penetration looked deep, but the rest didn't look as bad. Dennis's eyelid was bleeding, but I wasn't sure if the eye itself had been cut. At least he was still breathing.

I hopped over to the knife, knelt down, and leaned backwards. Sweat poured down my body faster than the rain outside as my still-shackled hands reached down for the knife. It took several tries, and I thought I heard Jasper groan. Finally, I grabbed the knife handle. Fortunately for me, Jasper kept everything in prime condition. The knife was very sharp and quickly cut through my bonds. Unfortunately, Jasper was coming around and my hands were still cuffed and I had no idea where the key was.

My feet were free when Jasper shook his head groggily. I stepped quickly over, balanced myself carefully, and aimed a kick at his crotch with all the power I could muster. He shrieked nearly as loudly as Dennis. He groaned and arched his body in agony, then pulled himself into a fetal position. I needed him unconscious. Dead would not have bothered me. I aimed a kick at his kidneys, and he flopped onto his back with his hands in front of his running shorts. His head was close enough to the wall. I aimed a kick at it. His skull thunked resoundingly against the wood, and his eyes closed in unconsciousness.

I glanced at Roy, still eagerly waiting to use his fangs if anybody got too close. He seemed securely in place. I had no experience with poisonous creatures. Trying to kill it could just as easily get me bitten.

Anal-retentive insane people are good for one thing. In one of the drawers I found sets of keys, each in its own little receptacle, neatly labeled. With my wrists still shackled I couldn't reach far enough into the drawer to pick up the correct key. I had to dump the contents out, but I managed to do this with some care so they didn't spill all over. Still, it was good that I remembered what the key looked like. It took painful contortions, and I scraped off large chunks of my wrists before I got the key inserted, turned, and freed myself.

First, I shackled Jasper with handcuffs and rope. Then I hurried to Dennis. Blood still oozed, especially from the last cut, but I didn't bother trying to clean the wounds. Infection was the least of my worries. I covered his face with a towel and hoped he would stay unconscious until I got us some help. My watch told me we'd been captive for over three hours.

I took the car keys from Dennis's pocket. I wedged the shotgun under his belt and stuffed the handgun into my pants pocket. I didn't see any other weapons, nor could I waste time looking for them. I didn't doubt Jasper had an arsenal handy.

Outside, the rain fell in torrents and the sky was dark. The mud squished under my feet as I carried Dennis through the downpour to the car. While in the cabin I'd dried off some, but I was completely soaked again before I'd walked three feet. The path was more mud and puddles than solid ground. I had to plant each foot carefully in front of me so I wouldn't slip. Even then, halfway to the car, I almost dropped Dennis. A large tree was in the direction of my fall and stopped me, but I had to go to one knee to keep myself up. As I staggered forward again, a bolt of lightning sheared through the top of a mammoth pine tree about twenty yards ahead.

While struggling through the downpour, I wondered what to do with Jasper. I remembered the description he'd given of the effect of a bite from a cottonmouth. He was young and strong, so it might take quite a while for the bite to kill him, but even so I was sure that if he didn't receive prompt medical attention he would die. Not being an anal-retentive loony but a man desperate for escape, I had not cleaned after myself. The knives and keys were as available to him as they had been to me. I figured our safety was more important than his life. I decided to go back to at least throw his means of getting loose into the surrounding swamp. I would get us out of danger, then send help back to him. By the time I eased Dennis into the car and closed the door, I knew what I had to do. I couldn't just let Jasper die. I took both shotgun and handgun and turned back to the cabin.

Jasper stood at the edge of sight in the trees. For once I wished I was the neatnik in my relationship with Scott. A little more anal retentiveness and I'd have cleaned away Jasper's means of freeing himself.

Jasper raised a hand with a gun in it and came running toward me. I dropped the handgun, grabbed the shotgun, pulled it up, and fired both barrels. The echoes rivaled the thunder for dominance. Jasper disappeared into the foliage. I didn't know if I'd hit him or not and I didn't want to take any chances. I grabbed the handgun, jumped in the car, started the engine, and realized I was facing the wrong way. I had neither room nor time to turn around.

I glanced out the windshield. Jasper emerged from the undergrowth and began running toward us. I threw the engine into first and aimed the car at him. I grabbed the handgun, reached outside the window, and fired two rounds. My ears rang from the noise.

When he saw the gun, Jasper threw himself onto the ground and rolled into cover. I slammed on the brake and jammed the car into reverse. The car fishtailed in the mud. Jasper's arm and head appeared around a tree fifteen feet away. He started firing. I tromped my foot down on the accelerator as the sound of gunfire boomed and roared. It's tough enough to hit something that is standing still, and a moving target is even more difficult. Maybe if I repeated this to myself often enough, it would come true.

Because I was racing backward, I had to grip the wheel tightly with both hands to keep from flying off the road. I'd never driven backwards so far, so fast, much less in such conditions. Not something a lot of us practice.

Jasper was now maybe fifty feet away. Of course, a Volkswagen is a mite or two bigger than a person; but large as it was, we were throwing up showers of spray as we bounded over the ruts and potholes, making accuracy even tougher.

Even if I dared take a hand off the wheel, I hesitated about firing the gun. I had no more ammunition for the shotgun and didn't know how many rounds I had left in the handgun. I had to assume Jasper had an unlimited supply.

Using the side and rearview mirrors for guidance made me keep my head further above the protection of the dashboard than I wanted, but there was no helping it; I had to see our path. The VW's engine was in the back; so except for a tire, which wouldn't have stopped me at this point, the only vital thing Jasper could hit was my exposed head.

I was going faster than I should have on the muddy road. Jasper began to sprint toward us. As the tires slipped in the mud, so did Jasper's footing. He fell twice, and the second time came up limping. Trying to run and limp and shoot made his aim even more inaccurate. Forget this movie crap where they raise their guns and make dead-aim shots after swinging their guns into position. Nevertheless, we weren't far enough away. The windshield shattered from one of the shots.

Then his firing abruptly stopped. Was he reloading, or circling around, or planning a trick, or finally being overcome by snake venom? I had no idea.

I came to the end of the small lane we'd entered last. Finally, there was enough room to maneuver. I swung the car around, rammed the clutch into first, and floored it. The wheels spun in the mud for an agonizing instant. I eased up on the gas pedal. The car rocked back. I gunned the engine again and the car surged forward.

The only thing I can liken to that journey back to the road is Mr. Toad's wild ride. I concentrated on holding on to the wheel, seeing through the rain, and not missing any turns. My thoughts swung wildly through anger and vengeance to memories of Scott and my family to moving to an arid desert and thinking I'd kiss every flat inch of the Midwest if I ever got back to Illinois.

Except for the final turn, we'd taken every right to get in, so now I took every left to get out. I had no idea how far we had to go. Getting here had taken at least forty-five minutes.

Thunder boomed all around us, and I could see streaks of lightning through the thick foliage. Rain poured in through the broken windshield. The only thing wetter I could imagine would be drowning in the ocean. It was odd driving in the rain without wipers.

After one sharp turn, for which I had to slow, I thought I saw in the distance a solid gray spot that could have been the highway. Seconds later I realized that it was Jasper in the middle of the road. I hunched down, tried to swerve the car from side to side as much as I dared, yet aim straight toward him. Again his gun boomed amid the rain. He must have hit the front of the car any number of times, but I held on, barely keeping my eyes above the rim of the dashboard. Several shots whizzed through the broken windshield and smashed through the rear window.

When I was twenty feet from him, Jasper moved off the path and behind a screen of brush. He could simply wait by the side of the road and pour a rain of fire into the car as we passed. I picked up the handgun and aimed it out the front window. Driving forward and gripping the wheel with one hand would have to work. I slowed for an instant. I wrenched the wheel toward the farther side of the road. Water spewed from the tires on the right side of the car. I saw Jasper grinning as he raised his gun. Suddenly I swung the car toward him, accelerated, and began firing. The bushes swayed violently as we rushed past. The car began to swerve. I swung the wheel violently to the left. The car swayed and then rocked back onto the road. I floored it. Gunshots roared next to my ear. I heard them thunking into the car, but we flew on. Unfortunately, now, for the first time, he would have a shot at the engine.

Gunfire continued behind us. White smoke began to shoot from the rear as I drove on. Seconds later we came to the row of weeping willows that had marked our entrance into the swamp. I plowed through their dangling branches and turned back toward Brinard.

Dennis woke up a mile or so down the road. He variously screeched and moaned, "I'm going to die! . . . I'm going to be blind! . . . God, it hurts! . . . God, I'm sorry! . . . Make it stop! . . . Please, let me die!" I tried to comfort him as best I could, with one hand on the wheel and the other patting and caressing him.

Mercifully, he passed out again a few minutes before the smoke stopped pouring out of the back of the car. Seconds later the warning lights on the dashboard lit up. I didn't care if I drove the car with hazard lights brighter than the lightning around us. However, on the next rise, the car began to lose power. Down the next decline we picked up speed, but the next incline was impossible. The car coughed, shuddered, and stopped in the middle of the road.

Two cars had passed us going the other way; none had caught up and passed us going this way. I got out and hurried to the passenger side. I had no idea what resources Jasper might have. Perhaps even now he and his favorite tank were rumbling toward us. I wasn't going to feel safe until I was in the middle of some kind of civilization. I opened the door, made sure Dennis was breathing, and carefully lifted him from the car.

I began to carry Dennis. I was halfway up the next incline when I heard a car engine behind us. I turned. I didn't know if it would be Jasper in full pursuit or a stranger willing to help. It turned out to be neither. An old man in a straw hat glanced at us once and accelerated over the rise.

I started forward again. I was almost to the top of the hill when a police car topped the rise in front of us. I saw the brake lights flash on. The car skidded until it was half off the road. Using the shoulder, the driver righted the car, turned around, flipped on the Mars lights, and parked behind us. Cody hurried over.

"What the hell?" was his only question. Then he saw how badly hurt Dennis was. Quickly he helped me carry him to the backseat of the police car. I flopped into the front. I barely noticed the cool air flowing from the vents. I realized how drenched I was and then noticed that my hands and arms were trembling worse than a junkie in need of a fix.

8

Despite the humidity, I continued to shiver. We used both the blankets from the trunk on Dennis. I wrapped my arms around myself. Cody put the heat on. We kept the windows open wide enough for fresh air but closed enough to keep out the rain. He radioed ahead so they would be ready for us at the emergency-room entrance when we got to the hospital.

"How'd you happen to be on the road?" I asked.

"Violet insisted I at least check the road to the swamp. She can be pretty persuasive. She got worried when you didn't come back."

As we raced toward Brinard, I told him what had happened. I did not relate all the leads Jasper had given us about who might want to kill the sheriff. I did ask, "What's the story on Jasper's dad? How could he protect an insane son?"

"Lots of tolerance for eccentricity in the South."

"Violet said the same thing the other night. This isn't eccentric—this is stark raving, totally, entirely, certifiably nuts."

"His dad owns more than half that swamp. Jasper lives there legally. The family was one of the first to settle the county. They've got cash and history on their side."

Our trip was slowed by the elements. By the time we were halfway to the hospital, Dennis was shivering and sweating. He became conscious enough to begin moaning. If nothing else, the shock and loss of blood could kill him.

After several miles of silence I asked, "Did the autopsy report come back on the sheriff?"

"Yes."

"What did it say?"

"He wasn't killed there. We've only identified your fingerprints so far. He had a mild narcotic in his system."

"He was given knockout drops?"

"Probably. Enough of something to make him sleepy and easy to control, happy and goofy."

"He died laughing. Good for him. Where was he the night before?"

"Wife says he left at eleven. He told her he had police business to take care of. She didn't ask. As sheriff he was always on call, no matter what the hour. If something came up that needed a decision or was a major problem, his orders were to call him in."

"Was there a real police call that night?"

"We haven't been able to confirm one. They found his car in the middle of the forest. None of your fingerprints so far."

"So he was out cavorting in the countryside at all hours on any given night."

"Sometimes there really was police business to do."

"And I'm the Easter bunny."

"I thought you were the good fairy." The man had a little bit of a sense of humor.

"Has anybody tried to figure out what he was doing or where he went that night?"

"I haven't heard anything."

"Nobody's asked. Somebody must have seen him."

"If they did, they haven't come forward."

"Jasper talked like he was best buddies with at least one person in the police department."

"That's hard for me to believe."

"Not for me. I'd suspect the police department would be a good place to find Klan members, or Nazis, or skinheads."

"The guys are okay. Jasper was too crazy. Nobody would hang around with him."

"Who on the department would be most likely to want to join Jasper in a group?"

"Nobody." I couldn't tell if he was covering up or just being loyal to his own, which could have been the same thing.

"What killed him, officially?"

"A dull and rusty razor blade. Whoever did it kept cutting after he was dead. Report said it wasn't just a quick slit. Somebody had to saw away for at least a little while."

"Somebody was very angry. Did he struggle?"

"No evidence of it. You saw the body. No tissue under his nails. Gun with bullets in it just sitting there on his hip."

"He must have made a lot of people very angry." I thought I knew the names of some of them. I wanted to talk to the people Jasper had mentioned as soon as possible.

On the outskirts of Brinard I said, "I know you don't have to answer this, and I'm not trying to make you angry, but why do you dance in front of guys? It can't be just the money. As a cop in this town, wouldn't you be able to get a reasonably decent part-time job?"

He rubbed his chin and shifted in his seat. "I'm straight."

"I'm not disputing that."

"The money is unbelievably good. I'm in good shape. I work out a lot at home. I feel like a stud when I do a strip. It's a trip to have people watch me naked."

"Why not work in front of women in one of those exotic places I saw signs for on the highway?"

"Our good southern women can take their clothes off in them, but they can't go there to watch a man take off his."

"What about afterwards, when you leave with guys?"

He looked at me carefully. We were a block away from the hospital parking lot. He said, "I just lay there. I let them do what they want, but they know the rules. No kissing. I don't touch them."

"You don't enjoy it even a little?"

"I lay there and think about women and having an orgasm. I concentrate on that."

If it worked for him, who was I to disagree? He had his reality all rationalized and in comfortable pigeonholes in his mind.

At the emergency-room entrance, they rushed Dennis in.

A small cluster of reporters, including one television minicam, formed a crowd around me. When Cody called the hospital, someone must have been listening to the police band on the radio and tipped them off.

The reporters flung questions at me. I marched to the doors leading to the emergency room and followed Dennis in. Cody kept the reporters out of the unit.

I called up to the CCU. Mary, Shannon, and Mrs. Carpenter were there. Scott had left to find Violet and to hunt for me. The hospital personnel brought me some dry clothes. Taking off my wet garments was a joy. Drying off was heavenly. I put on white hospital orderly pants and a letterman's jacket from the lost and found. I'd had a choice of that or a Bullwinkle sweatshirt, which I'd have taken except it was three sizes too small.

They rushed Dennis into surgery. They insisted I lie on a gurney and be examined in the emergency room. The nurse took my temperature and blood pressure. I was exhausted, desperately in need of sleep and a warm blanket. If somebody suggested a trip across the Sahara for our next vacation, I'd have leapt at the idea. A heaping gallon of chocolate-chip-cookie-dough ice cream smothered in tons of hot chocolate syrup would not have been amiss, either. I was too keyed up to rest. I had the goods on half the county. I wasn't planning to rest until several people gave satisfactory answers.

Dr. McLarty came in to examine me. Good. One of the people on my list. He poked, prodded, asked me where it hurt, and declared me to be fine. He seemed clinical and distant, not like the kindly local practitioner who'd spoken softly and at great length with the Carpenter family about their father.

He did ask what happened. Telling him the physical stuff in this antiseptic surrounding caused me to begin shaking again. Not enough time and distance had passed to begin to diminish the horror of the situation. He saw me shivering, called for the nurse, and directed her to bring me a blanket.

The nurse brought in several. She and McLarty gently wrapped me in three layers of warmth. The nurse left.

I felt myself stop shaking. I eyed McLarty as he made notes on my chart. He sat on a stool with four legs with wheels on the ends.

"How's Dennis?" I asked.

"They're still working on him," McLarty said. "They think the eye should be fine. The lid got sliced, but that's all."

"He's a great kid."

McLarty sat at a small desk and finished filling out hospital forms.

I said, "Dennis said you wanted to talk to me. Do you have information about the sheriff that might help me find his murderer?"

He put down his pen and rotated the chair so that he

faced me. He folded his arms across his chest and crossed his ankles.

"It must be nice," he said. "Living in Chicago, prancing around in the gay pride parade . . ."

"What the hell does that have to do with anything? That does it! Nobody else in this town gets to say another nasty thing about my being gay. Not you. Not anybody. If you have something useful to say that will help me discover who killed the sheriff, fine. Otherwise shut the fuck up and keep your bigoted opinions to yourself."

"I'm gay," he said.

What was I supposed to say to that: "Okay, since you're gay you can have bigoted opinions"?

"Then why start out with an attack on me?"

"Because I'm envious and jealous. You've got a beautiful lover, a famous baseball player, and every gay man on the planet would give anything to be in your position. Yet you two come down here and stir things up. The rest of us have to live here."

"I didn't 'stir things up.' They were pretty well boiling when I got here. I still don't get your problem."

"I just want to live a quiet life. Not bother anybody. My mother and aunt are here. I can't leave. I have to stay here to care for them. You running around town flaunting the fact that you're gay just upsets everybody. I'm the 'bachelor' in town. I know they whisper about me, but I don't want my mother to know."

"You really don't think she knows you're gay?"

"I never press the issue."

I shook my head. "You told Dennis you wanted to talk to me."

"I don't usually work in the ER, but with the rain we've had a lot of accidents. However, I took your case deliberately. I wanted to ask you to tone down your behavior, if not for the sake of the few gay people in town, then to warn you that bad things could happen."

I glanced down at the blankets I was wrapped in. "Gosh, you were right. Congratulations."

He frowned. "I don't think sarcasm helps."

"Do you have information that might help me find out who killed the sheriff?"

"If I tell you anything, I cannot have my name associated with you in the paper. Talking in here this long could begin to look suspicious."

"Somebody has a stopwatch timing visits with each patient? This is absurd. What do you know?"

"If this got out, I could be drummed out of the profession."

I waited.

"The sheriff came to me four times in the past five years to be treated for sexually transmitted diseases."

"Did he have AIDS?"

"He was tested. No. These were the run-of-the-mill, garden-variety, cheating-on-your-wife kind."

"She never knew?"

He shrugged.

"Why didn't he go out of town to be tested?"

"He knew I'd keep quiet. He figured out I was gay and threatened to expose me."

"How can you live like that?"

He unfolded his arms from his chest, reached a hand up under his glasses, and began to massage the bridge of his nose. When done, he said, "I just do."

"If you're the 'bachelor' in town, what difference does it make if he tells everybody you're gay?"

"You don't understand."

"No, I don't."

"People might think I'm gay, but unless I have naked lovers dancing in my front yard, they can ignore it. I can be

146

friendly Dr. McLarty. If it's out in the open, then something has to be done about it. Preachers have to make statements, the bigots in town have to fling slurs and become physically violent. Silence equals survival."

He gazed at me evenly. His life was a chilling one that I would never want to live, but I suspected it was all too common among too many gays and lesbians. I wasn't going to change him or the people with narrow minds by berating the compromises he'd made to live his life. I switched topics.

"From whom did the sheriff catch the diseases?"

"He wouldn't tell me. I always guessed it was women he picked up at the Rebel Hell."

"Did his wife catch any of the infections?"

"He claimed they never had sex after he slept with other women and before he got tested."

"You believed that?"

"I wasn't in a position to challenge what he said. If she was ill, she never came to me for treatment. The gossip in town never included them having fights in public."

"Where were you the night he was killed?"

"Home, alone, in bed, asleep."

"Any other gay people in town it would do me any good to talk to? Any that might have been afraid of him and could have information? Maybe had a temper and might have wanted to kill him?"

"I'll question people, not you. There aren't many of us, and we have to be very careful. If anybody knows anything, I'll let you know."

I thanked him. I felt warmer, so I took off the blankets. Now, I wanted to see Scott more than anything else. I also wanted to find some food.

I found Scott pacing the floor in the CCU. "I just got here," he said after he hugged me. "Are you all right? What's happened? Where are your clothes?"

"Doctor says I'm okay. We went out to see loony Jasper in his swamp. The reporter I was with is in surgery."

Violet walked off the elevator. "You're safe!" she said. "What about Dennis?"

"They're operating. I'm hungry. I'll give you both all the details over a hot meal."

On the way out of the hospital I asked Scott, "Is your dad okay?"

"Yes. He might be able to walk a little tomorrow. We're very hopeful. What happened?"

I insisted on Della's Bar-b-que. Violet found out which door of the hospital the reporters were clustered around and we left by another exit. Outside, the rain continued to pelt down. With any luck the entire state would wash away.

The restaurant was nearly empty, but we sat in a booth far in the back, partly to be as unseen as possible, certainly to be unheard. Sometimes paranoids do have enemies, and we had a shitload of them.

I told the whole story as we ate. Food had never tasted so good to me. The streetlights came on and total dark fell before I finished relating all of the horrors of the afternoon.

Scott sat on the same side of the booth as me. He put his arm around me to comfort me. I didn't care if the whole goddamn town was staring and taking pictures.

"I can believe that hypocrite Hollis is molesting kids," Scott said. "I can't believe he gets away with it."

"If he really did it," Violet said. "You only have Jasper's word for any of this."

"But I'm going to try and prove all of it," I said.

"Poor Dennis," Violet said.

"We should do something for him," I said.

Scott said, "I probably have a few friends left in the

media. There's got to be a job somewhere other than around here. When all this is over, I'll try talking to a few people."

"Good idea," Violet said.

"And we're leaving town," Scott said.

"I can't," I said. "I'm still a suspect in the sheriff's murder."

"I'm calling our lawyer. Todd must know some way to get you out of here."

"I'm going to want to talk to everybody that Jasper told me about, including your family."

"None of my brothers or sisters would do anything to hurt me."

Violet said, "Maybe I can speak subtly with Hiram and Shannon. Not get them upset. I can at least try. We have to find out what Jasper was talking about."

"They wouldn't do anything," Scott insisted. "I'll go with you to do the other questioning. Dad's doing much better and I can get away for a while."

I told them about the police reports that Cody had told me about. Violet had also talked to him, and he had given her the same information.

"Why a rusty razor blade?"

"Wouldn't killing him that way take longer?" Scott asked.

"It makes it more vicious and angry. Jasper fits that mold. This is a very unhappy person," Violet said.

"I wouldn't call Jasper unhappy," I said. "He was a raving loony."

"What's wrong with him must have started somewhere," Scott said.

Violet shook her head, "Some people are just plain crazy from the day they're born. No reason for it. Nothing anybody can do. Maybe Jasper's parents were kind and loving;

maybe they beat him every night. We'll probably never know. There isn't always a rational explanation for everything."

"Hard to picture a killer coming out of a stable and loving home," Scott said.

I thought of his siblings and kept my mouth shut.

"What if the things Jasper told you aren't true?" Violet asked. "Maybe the preacher doesn't molest children. Certainly I've never heard of such a thing. A whole town couldn't keep that quiet. I don't think they'd want to. I hope they wouldn't."

"I'm going to work on the basis that what he said was true. Somebody had to have a reason to kill the sheriff, and these are good ones."

"Is Jasper still alive?" Violet asked.

"Cops said they'd look for him," I said, "but I guess they'll wait for the rain to stop before going into the swamp."

"From what you said he sounds pretty resourceful," Scott said. "Maybe we should take precautions."

"Like call the police?" I asked. "Excuse me, you're both from here, and I don't mean to be insulting, but I don't trust the local cops in the least. We've got one who is less than happy with us because we're blackmailing him for information, and one of them who was at least as much of a Nazi as Jasper. I think we'd best just be extremely careful."

Violet said, "I talked with Leota, Peter's wife. She hasn't got a clue about why her husband died. You can cross her off the list."

"We've got to get some answers," Scott said. "You've been through enough, Tom."

"Don't do something foolish," Violet said.

"I'm going to do what is necessary to clear Tom's name."

As we got ready to leave, Violet said, "I can't go with you. I've got to get back to the library. The water in Johnson Creek is starting to rise pretty rapidly. We're moving some of the books and audiovisual equipment to higher ground."

"Is it going to flood?" I asked.

"Weather report said it had been raining about an inch every two hours," Violet said. "We've had over three inches. They claim it will stop some time tonight, but I'm not going to take any chances. Low-lying areas are going to be swamped. Good thing it's been so dry this year. I've got all the employees and lots of volunteers over at the library, and I want to be on hand to give directions."

Thunder, lightning, and pouring rain met us outside. Violet gave us directions to all the people we were supposed to see.

"I want to talk to Preacher Hollis first," I said. "If he's diddling little girls, we've got a powerful tool to hold over his head."

"He has to be reported and stopped," Scott said.

"We'll hold it over his head tonight and report it first chance we get after that."

Scott still had his rented BMW.

As we got in, we saw the television truck go by with the letters WRIS and a smiling peach as a logo on the side. We ducked down until it passed us.

We drove past the jail and the police department. We crossed over a bridge about forty feet long. The street lights glinted off the surface of the swollen river. It still looked like it had quite a way to go before it reached the level of the bridge. A slight slope led from the banks of the stream on both sides. It would have to rise at least fifteen feet above the banks to get to the jail. I looked around. If it got that high, a sizable chunk of the town would be under water.

Preacher Hollis and his family lived next to his church about a mile from downtown. A light shone through a stained-glass window in the nave of the church that soared above the towering trees around it. Bright lights lit up the empty parking lot, and a covered breezeway that led to a two-story school behind the church. Their house was behind this. All the buildings were built of dark red brick. As we pulled up to the house, I looked back and saw a streak of lightning illuminate the cross on top of the spire.

We dashed through the rain to the front door. A gray-haired woman in a blue smock responded to our knock. If she recognized us, she didn't say anything. When we asked for the preacher, she asked us to wait. She shut the door most of the way and left. The door reopened a minute later to reveal a pudgy man with black hair and a big smile, which died as soon as he saw us. He wore a flower print shirt, fluorescent Bermuda shorts, and black socks with no shoes. If nothing else, a call to the fashion police was in order.

"Can I help you gentlemen?" he asked. "Could I hope you've come to confess your sin?" The smile began to return to his face.

"We need to talk to you about the sheriff's death," I said.

The man's face turned purple.

Scott wrenched open the screen and caught the wooden front door before Preacher Hollis could finish slamming it. Scott followed his fist into the house. I trailed after.

"Hey, you can't come in here like this! Millie, call the police!" The woman reached for the phone.

"Please call," I said. "The whole world will want to hear what we have to say."

Millie stopped with her finger above the buttons on the phone.

"Preacher, we're going to talk about your activities with little girls."

"I beg your pardon."

"Specifically, when you have sex with children."

Millie let out a piercing scream and fled the room.

I thought, She knows it's true.

He looked after his wife, then back at us. "This is utter nonsense."

"People aren't going to like it when their professional Christian and resident holy man is a pedophile. They might be even more angry with you than they are at us."

Preacher Hollis strode toward us. His little piggy eyes glared out of his gleaming pink face. He stuck the smirk on his face that so many of the righteous present to the world. "I'll destroy the both of you. We preachers will make sure Mr. Carpenter's baseball career is ruined. He will be too frightened to ever pitch in a major-league ballpark. The righteous will not permit it."

"Oh, blow it out your ass," I said. I plunked myself down on the couch. The furniture was in shades of pale green, accented with brass pole lamps.

"Our source says he has pictures of you."

Hollis turned stark white. He breathed deeply for several moments, then rallied. "Impossible. I never touched anyone. Get out of my house!"

"How did the sheriff find out?" I asked.

"I don't know what you're talking about."

"Yeah, you do. And so does your wife. Why don't we go through the list of little trips you've taken with members of your congregation and talk to all the little girls who were there? Someone will tell the truth. Did the sheriff demand money, or simply permanent support for his reelections?"

This was all bluff based on the testimony of someone I thought was certifiably insane and hopefully dead.

"You'd better leave," he said. "No one in my congregation would talk to you."

"Only takes one."

We didn't hear any more about calling the police. That, as much as his wife's actions, made me believe he was guilty. An innocent man calls the cops and doesn't try to trade bluff for bluff.

I said, "I don't want to tell anyone about your little escapades. I just want to know where you were two nights ago and what compromise you reached with the sheriff."

"I was here."

"Now, now, we could use the phone to call the reporters. You've heard there's a pack of them in town to cover Tom and Scott, the evil faggots."

"Leave!"

Scott stooped to the phone, picked up the receiver, and handed it to me.

I punched 411. I listened to the rings on the line. "Who do I ask for first? We did see that WRIS television truck. Let's call them first. They local or out of Atlanta?" The preacher seemed disinclined to be helpful. I asked for the number of the station. The operator told me the signal came out of Macon. I said the number out loud and let the recording repeat itself. I didn't think the preacher'd lend me a pencil and paper. I had nothing in my pockets but my sodden wallet. I still had the outfit on that I'd gotten in the hospital. I began punching in the number.

Preacher Hollis rushed across the room and wrenched the phone out of my hand.

"You can't," he said. "I'm sixty years old. Even if it's not true, and it isn't, that kind of allegation ruins someone's reputation. You must stop."

"Give us information."

"I admit nothing," he said. "But to stop you from making these false accusations, I will say that I did see the sheriff two nights ago."

"What time?"

"Just after midnight. I'd been to see a member of the congregation late. We'd prayed for her son, who is a drug addict. Earlier in the day the sheriff told me to meet him at midnight at Magnolia's in Filmore County."

Scott said, "That's the next county south. I know Magnolia's. It's got a worse reputation than Rebel Hell."

Hollis said, "He told me he knew what you said you know. Again, I wanted to avoid a scandal."

"What did he make you promise?"

"That I would support him in every election and oppose Clara. That I had to get behind all his projects."

We left with the nugget of knowledge of where the sheriff had started out his evening.

"Are we really not going to tell?" Scott asked as we got in the car.

"Let's stop at the hospital, dodge some reporters, and check on your dad. Then we'll call Todd, get him working on getting me out of town, and let him decide how to handle the preacher scandal. I have no qualms about breaking my word and ratting on him. Using a power position to destroy the lives of little kids is the most disgusting thing I can think of. Todd'll know if they have to get the state police in here or the FBI. They'll have to investigate and find someone to talk."

Half an hour later we were on the road south to Filmore County and Magnolia's.

"How do you know about all these places?" I asked. "I thought you were the saintly athlete, too busy practicing or working out or being a star to have heard about these dens of iniquity."

"I used to hang out in the parking lot of the Piggly Wiggly on Saturday nights with the other kids. On hot summer evenings we'd sneak off and go places. Popular athletes get taken everywhere. We have a secret society that lets us in on all the hidden knowledge—a sort of fraternity of with-it kids who know about sex and booze and the secrets of adult life before everyone else."

"Bullshit."

"Sounded good to me."

"I played sports in high school and college. We just pretty much hung out and drank."

"Sort of the same here. I went to Magnolia's once. Me and Peter and a few guys—I think Hiram was with us. We figured we could get in. Didn't think they'd say no to teen-age stud athletes. During the trip down we bragged about how often we'd been laid, and how we were going to get laid that night."

"All true?"

"Mostly lies."

"What happened?"

"They threw us out."

We passed through numerous small towns. There wasn't much traffic on the road. It was late on a Thursday night, and it had been raining. We drove around large puddles of standing water on the road.

"Where is this place?" I asked.

"A mile or two into Thomas Jefferson Forest, going in from the south entrance. No direct way from here—we'll have to go around."

We turned off the main road ten feet past a sign that read, "Grandma's Launderette—Free Dry on Thursdays." It looked like the sign had been there since the Civil War, but I didn't see any building to correspond.

"Where's Grandma's?" I asked.

"Sign's been there since I was a kid. Used to be able to see a foundation for a building about thirty feet into the woods."

We drove down a road that must not have been used since Sherman marched through these parts. We plopped into water-filled potholes and banged over and into lumps and bumps. The expensive car did its best to ease our path, but a new set of shocks would probably be in order when we turned it back in. Time and again water sluiced up the side of the car, caking it with mud that was quickly washed off by the rain.

We topped a small rise. Down the other side, I saw a ten-foot-wide expanse of rushing water racing directly across our path.

"You're not going through that?" I asked.

"I don't remember any deep ravines on this road. It's just a bitty crick most of the time. Can't be that deep."

"Yes it can."

"Conventional wisdom at times like this is, If the car starts to float downstream, abandon it."

"Nobody's going to be at the bar tonight. I vote we turn around."

"Will you calm down? Everything is going to be fine. Plus the next step in the trail leads down this road. You want to wait until morning?"

Our headlights illuminated the pouring rain and the swollen creek. I put my hand on the door handle.

"Do I shut or open my eyes?"

"We'll be fine."

I kept the door open a crack as we crossed. I figured this way we could jump out of the car if it started to float away. The water barely got up to our hubcaps.

I hate it when he's right.

A few minutes later we pulled up in front of a shack that made the Rebel Hell look like a palace. A feeble light shone over the door. A yellow neon sign in one window said "Magnolia's." Those and our car lights were it as far as evidence of rural electrification were concerned. The roof of the place sagged, gutters hung half off the two sides of the building I could see, and the wooden walls seemed to bulge outward. In one flash of lightning I thought I caught sight of an outhouse. Three pickup trucks nuzzled up to the walls, and at the far end of the lot was a van that seemed to be sinking into the mud.

We pulled as close to the building as we could and dashed through the rain to the door. Inside, directly across from us, was a bar that ran the length of that side of the room. It seemed to have been made of the same warped wood as the walls. Black-and-white photos of cowboys at rodeos were crammed around all the edges of a smoke-begrimed mirror, which reflected the interior. A thin strand of Christmas lights lined the ceiling on three sides. Two revolving beer ads provided the only other brightness in this part of the bar. To the right were three Formica-topped tables, each of which had enough grime encrusted on top to qualify as an individual toxic dump. A warped linoleum dance floor was just beyond them. To the left was a beautiful pool table: dark green felt encased by dark mahogany. A hanging Tiffany lamp above the table gave off the most light in the whole bar.

Three guys holding pool cues and smoking cigars looked up at us. Their glare was unfriendly. Picture three guys too ugly for even an MTV video: tight tank-top T-shirts emphasizing scrawny bodies; scruffy, unshaven, pockmarked faces; unwashed hair hanging in strands to below their shoulders; and random streaks of unwashed grime on their shoulders, necks, and faces.

Behind the bar was a tall, attractive African-American woman. She wore a starched white blouse and tight blue jeans that emphasized her sensuous figure.

We approached the bar and sat down on black-vinyl-topped stools.

The woman strolled over to us and asked, "What can I get for you boys?" Her voice was beautifully melodious and sensuous. She could sing for any opera company or drive a client wild in a scented boudoir.

We ordered two beers. She served them, then said, "Hell of a night to be outdoors."

"We need information," I said.

I looked in the mirror behind her. Through the murk I could see the three men who'd been playing pool, arrayed in a semicircle behind us.

9

Scott jerked around on his stool and grabbed the nearest man's pool cue. Scott leapt right and I jumped left so we would be able to come at them from both sides. Scott bashed the pool cue against the bar. Half broke off, twirled through the air, crashed through the window, and broke the neon "Magnolia" sign. The other portion Scott brandished under the nose of the nearest menacing figure.

One of them grabbed a beer bottle by the top and smashed off the bottom against a table. The one with the world's ugliest goatee held on to his pool cue as if it were a baseball bat. Unfortunately for my sense of prejudice, none of them wore bib overalls. Nor did any of them grin and reveal a snaggletooth.

A voice behind us said, "That's going to cost you, son."

Out of the corner of my eye I saw the African-American woman holding a sawed-off shotgun aimed at Scott's back. She swung it slowly toward the three attackers. The woman said, "Go."

Seconds later, they were gone.

"Thank you," I said.

"You owe me two hundred bucks for the window, the neon, and the pool cue," she said. "This is my place. You bust it up, you got to pay up."

160

"You're Magnolia?"

"Yep. I'll take plastic for payment."

I gave her my Visa card. As she wrote up the bill, I asked, "Why were they so hostile?"

"Sheriff Woodall's death is big news all over this part of the state," she said. "Mr. Carpenter's been famous since forever." She pointed at me. "Since the sheriff died, your face has been all over everywhere. Wouldn't be a baby in a hundred miles didn't know if you walked into a room. Sheriff was a big customer out here. People liked him. News about y'all as a couple is all over these parts. Folks are not happy about gay people in general, and you two are remarkably specific. Focuses their anger."

"How come you helped us?"

"This here is my place. It is not easy for an African-American woman to keep it running. I sympathize with you some, and not everyone in the South is a redneck bigot."

"We're trying to find out who really killed the sheriff. It's the only way I'm going to get out of here. We haven't had a lot of luck asking questions or getting help."

"I'll do what I can for y'all."

Lightning flashed through the broken window.

"Our last lead told us the sheriff came out here the night he was killed."

"Yep. He was here." She gave me my credit card back, leaned over the bar, and rested her elbows on the top. "Stayed for close on to an hour."

"Why haven't you told anyone this?"

"You're the first ones to come and ask. He was found in Brinard early in the morning. Far as I know his being here had no connection."

"Who'd he talk to? Did he do anything suspicious? Do you know where he went after? Did he leave with any-body?"

Her laughter rang out low and comfortable. "No wonder

everybody gets hostile at you. Too many questions coming too fast."

"I'm sorry," I said.

"That's all right—there's lotsa pressure on you. Let me see now. He talked to about everybody, and he did nothing suspicious. He didn't tell me where he was going. He left with . . ." She thought a minute. "I'm not sure I saw him when he left."

While we asked the next few questions, she plucked a hammer from under the bar, took some tacks and aluminum foil out of a drawer. When she was done tacking over the broken window, the rain ceased coming in. It also cut off any illumination from the lightning.

"We were told the sheriff often decided not to arrest women and took it out in trade instead. Maybe an angry husband or boyfriend, or a furious woman, decided to get even or put a stop to it."

She tapped her fingertips on the bar. "Rumors about that keep goin' round."

"Are they true?"

"A few of the women around here get together once in a while. We aren't radicals or anything. We're black and white women who meet to talk. It's very quiet and very secret. We haven't been able to do anything about the sheriff. We hear the same vague rumors. The only way to stop him is for somebody to be willing to stand up and accuse the bastard."

"No one will?"

"No one would. It isn't possible. The sheriff was very powerful. A woman would be admitting to being unfaithful to her husband. Still too many people around here who believe the woman is asking for it when she cries rape. Plus, word is he only does it to women who have committed a crime. He has that to hold over their heads as well. We've talked to several lawyers. Their hands were tied unless someone was willing to step forward."

"I'd like to be able to talk to some of those women," I said.

"I'm sorry. Even if I knew any names directly, I couldn't give them to you. We keep everybody's story confidential. We are sworn to secrecy. That helps make our group strong. Everybody knows that no one will tell. Opening up to you might help you, but it wouldn't help the women involved. I'm sorry."

I digested this refusal.

"How about husbands or boyfriends?" Scott asked. "Any of the men find out and try to get back at the sheriff?"

"I don't know of any."

"Preacher Hollis is the one who told us the sheriff was out here that night. We have information that Hollis was molesting little girls. We've got our lawyer in Chicago working on an investigation."

"Hollis? Far as I know he's simply a small-town fire-and-brimstone preacher. You sure about this? I can't picture him working up the nerve to touch his own prick. He's nothin' if not useless. None of the women have mentioned him, ever. Are you sure your information is right?"

"I don't know. Hollis was scared enough of us telling to admit he and the sheriff were here."

"He could have legitimately been afraid of that kind of scandal. Guilty or not, his career would be ruined."

"Was he here the other night?"

"Yes. And it wasn't the first time the preacher has come around. He's not supposed to be here. According to him, any place that serves liquor is an establishment straight from hell. He stays half an hour once in a while. He was here talking to the sheriff that night."

"If he wasn't afraid of blackmail, why would he come to meet the sheriff?"

"I don't know if they planned on meeting. When Hollis

shows up, he talks to a few people. Wasn't odd that he talked to the sheriff. They didn't seem to spend a lot of time together."

"If he's been molesting kids, I'd like to ruin his career."

"I do know that it won't take a lawyer from up north to get his ass if he's been molesting kids. If he's guilty, we'll bring him down, if I have to do the draggin' myself. Who told you this?"

I admitted it was Jasper Williams.

"That man is crazy. No reason on earth for a man to be that mean. He's the most evil person I have ever met. The only time I had to ask for help in the bar was to keep him away from here. Afterwards, he threatened to burn me out. Several times late at night, he followed me home in that old ragged Jeep he owns. Thing doesn't have any windows."

"How'd you get him to stop harassing you?"

She smiled. "Only way to deal with an insane man is to scare him more than he scares you. Ever hear of Hangin' Billy Joe Jones?"

Scott said, "Didn't he play nose tackle for a couple years in the pros? Made lots of neck tackles when he could, lot of late hits. Played for a bunch of teams. Too dirty even for the NFL."

"He lives in these parts. We're sort of friends."

"He paid a visit to Jasper's cabin?"

"Nobody is crazy enough to go there."

I admitted my foray earlier that day.

"And you lived to tell the tale? You always hear about people getting lost in the swamp and not coming out. Nobody knows anybody it happened to, but everybody has a cousin who has a friend who knows somebody who never came back."

Briefly I told the story.

"You were lucky," she said. "Even Hangin' Billy Joe Jones don't chance the swamp. He 'invited' Jasper over for a little visit to his house down in the woods. I don't know how he got him there or what he did when he got him there. I never asked. All I know is Jasper never came back here."

For a minute I listened to the thunder rumble around us. "Jasper also told us that Al Holcomb had an African-American mistress."

"Mister KKK dipping his wick in the forbidden fruit?"

"Do you know who the woman was?"

She hesitated an instant before she said no.

Her hesitation aroused my suspicions. Magnolia making it with the KKK? Didn't fit right, and I didn't think pressing her would do much good. If she wasn't going to tell, I had no way of making her.

She glanced around the bar. "It's not closing time, but I think I'm going to call it a night. Nobody's comin' out here anymore in this storm."

Scott and I proceeded to the door. Rain pelted down. One look at our car and I knew we weren't leaving in it. All four tires had been flattened. I looked back at Magnolia flipping switches and turning out the lights.

She walked over, saw the problem, and said, "Let's hope they left my van alone."

We dashed through the downpour. She flung herself into the driver's side. I sprang into the passenger seat and Scott leapt into the back. He closed the sliding door with a thud.

"You sure this thing runs?" I asked.

"Been through a couple of hurricanes down on the coast. We'll be fine." The motor gasped to life. The windshield wiper on my side barely cleared the water off the glass. She had to rock the van back and forth to ease it out of the rain-swollen ruts it was in. Magnolia may have gone as fast as five miles an hour on our way out. When we got to the crick, it looked a lot wider than it had when we crossed it the first time.

"Are we going to make it?" I asked.

She peered into the darkness left and right. "Lots of deaths in floods caused when people assume the road is still there. The water may not look high, but the road is totally gone."

"We made it through on the way in," Scott said.

"You were very foolish and very lucky," Magnolia said. She hitched the gearshift lever into reverse. "I know more than one way out of this forest."

For an hour we rattled through deep woods and pouring rain. Finally, we pulled onto the highway.

She drove us to Brinard. A hundred yards from the first lights of town, she slowed down and pulled to the side of the road.

"You boys will have to get out here."

"In the rain?" I asked.

"Why?" Scott asked.

"I have a reputation to keep. Saving your butts in my own place is one thing. Being seen driving you around is another. Folks still aren't too fond of black and white people hanging around together, as your buddy Al could tell you. I can only help you so far. I'll lend you an umbrella."

Scott and I trod down the side of the road, sharing the umbrella. The rain sluiced off the black covering. The wind was down at the moment, and the thunder and lightning seemed far off.

"This should be romantic," I said. "Hunched together in a pouring rain. We could do a little dance and sing and smile."

"All the world's a song cue."

"We can use the phone up ahead." I nodded toward the lights of the twenty-four-hour gas station in front of us.

The phone was outside but under an overhang. While Scott phoned, I decided to go inside and pick up something to eat.

Six pairs of eyes watched me approach the counter. A possible seventh pair belonged to an older man who, even from the back, looked like a reject from a Gabby Hayes look-alike contest. This guy was more shabbily dressed than any homeless person. He didn't turn around to look at me but kept growling at the clerk about his arthritis and the rain falling, the creek rising, and the gully washing.

When I stepped to the counter, pseudo-Gabby turned to look at me. He didn't wear a patch over one eye. This was good. Unfortunately, he had one glass eye. This was disconcerting. Then I realized I was being mean. The poor man had probably been maimed horribly in some accident and gone through life this way. I pictured Dennis being in the same position.

The old guy raised a beer can he was holding in his right hand. The top of the can had been removed, leaving jagged edges around the top. He blinked the one good eye at me, then spat a wad of tobacco juice into the can. He didn't miss a drop. Then he asked, "You the faggot we gonna lynch?"

Exit all sympathy stage left. I said, "I probably am."

He spat another wad of tobacco juice and grinned cheerfully, showing deeply stained dentures. He punched me playfully on the shoulder and said, "Can't wait. Haven't had a lynching since I was a lad. If the law gets to you first, it'll spoil all the fun."

"Not mine," I said. I put a sandwich and a bag of chips on the counter. The clerk made no move to ring them up.

I got the spit, grin, punch again from the old guy. I hoped he didn't screw up the sequence, or I could be drenched in brown goo.

"Lot of people powerful pissed at you. Heard Wainwright Richardson wants to lock you up. Whole rest of the county would just prefer to see you dead."

"How nice for them. I suppose I could try to get out of Dodge before sunup."

Spit, grin, punch.

"Almost like you maybe a little bit. Hope I get to be one of the boys at the hangin'."

I said to the clerk, "I'd like these items."

He still made no move to ring them up.

I looked around for Scott, who was still talking on the phone and not looking in this direction. The men in the group didn't surround me. They looked like everyday folks—ribbon clerks, assistant managers of the Piggly Wiggly, and maybe a guy who stocked shelves at the Winn Dixie. Their frowns and sneers declared them to be very unfriendly everyday folks, but they didn't seem the kind that would lynch me on the spot.

Gabby said, "You shouldn't ought to have come down here, and you surely shouldn't ought to have killed the sheriff."

I could have said, "Don't call me Shirley." I might have said, "Is this some cheap western?" But while I was only on the near side of nervous, I could be convinced to be scared. I did say, "Let's compromise. I'll leave and you guys can stand here and be prejudiced without me."

I turned around and walked out. I expected a squirt of tobacco juice in the back. I opened the door and ambled over to Scott. I thought he was arguing with someone. He slammed the phone down.

"Mary isn't around. I can't get anybody else in the family to come get us." He seemed near tears. "I talked to Nathan and I thought he understood about us, but I think Hiram and Shannon got to him. Son of a bitch."

"Let's try Violet." There was an actual phone book in the booth; you wouldn't find that anywhere in Chicago. I called Violet. She sounded like I woke her up, but she agreed to meet us. I didn't want to wait around, so we picked the library as a rendezvous point.

"Al Holcomb live around here?" I asked her.

"Two blocks out of your way." She gave me directions. She added, "I had a little meeting with Cody. He confirmed that Al has a black mistress."

"How did he know?"

"Said he had sources."

I said, "We'll stop and see Al before we meet you."

"At this hour?"

"Visiting the head of the Klan in the middle of the night works for me."

We huddled under the umbrella and marched to Al Holcomb's house. It was a three-story, narrow Victorian home with two turrets in front and filigree and detail on the woodwork under the roof and above the windows. We stood outside a screened-in porch. I leaned my thumb on the doorbell and let it bong. In a few minutes lights turned on inside the house. The lamp on the porch flicked on, but it took several moments for the front door to open.

The muzzle of a shotgun appeared in the opening, followed by Al Holcomb. "What do you want?" he demanded.

Gone was the overbearing good cheer from when I met him at Della's Bar-b-que.

"We need to talk to you," Scott said.

Holcomb pumped the shotgun. "I don't want to talk to you. Get off my property. I'll shoot you, and no jury will convict. I'll say you were trying to attack me. Remember what happened to that foreign kid in Louisiana? We know how to deal with visitors in the South." He stepped onto the porch and raised the gun to his shoulder.

"Why'd you kill the sheriff?" I asked. "Did he find out you have an African-American mistress?"

Slowly he lowered the shotgun to his side.

Hit it in one, I thought. "Can we talk?" I asked.

Thunder boomed and rain poured down around us.

He lifted the barrel of the gun with one hand and shoved it up against the hook holding the screen door closed. The hook thunked lightly against the wooden door. "I don't want to talk to you on the porch," he said. "I don't want people seeing me with you."

He stopped us three feet inside the front door. "I don't want you goin' no further." We were in a mud room, with umbrellas in a stand, boots on the floor, and raincoats on hooks. Doors led off to the left and directly ahead. To the right were stairs leading up.

"When did the sheriff find out you had an African-American mistress?"

"People are going to be sorry they talked to you," he said.

I hadn't thought about the capacity of the southern gentleman to get revenge on those around him. Maybe people who lived here could take care of themselves, but against the powers of the Klan and the velvet southern night, I wasn't sure.

"Jasper Williams told us first, but we've had it confirmed."

"By who?"

"The local cops, for one." We glared at each other.

"Most probably none of this would go anywhere if I kill you first."

"Even you can't be that stupid," I said. "Is this macho 'Kill everybody' crap real? You can't just indiscriminately murder people. Even in the South someone would notice dead bodies piling up."

He considered this for a minute.

I repeated my question. "When did the sheriff find out? We'll not spread it around, if you tell us the truth."

He sighed deeply.

"Couple weeks ago."

"How'd he find out?"

"I don't know. He had ways of finding out everything about this town."

"Why not go farther away for an affair? Atlanta? Nobody there would care about you or this little town."

"Who are you, Dear Abby? What's it to you where I went? What do you want?"

"What did the sheriff threaten you with?"

"I had to support him in all the elections. I had to oppose Clara and help find somebody to oppose her. He wanted her out of office."

"You one of the old boys who got Clara elected in the first place?"

"There's some of us in this county who try to take an interest in civic affairs. Somebody has to take responsibility, make tough decisions."

"That include being head of the Klan?"

"What's it to you?"

"If it was like the old days, my lover and I would have probably been lynched already."

"Don't be surprised if you still aren't. We don't like your kind in these parts."

"Where were you the night the sheriff was killed?"

"Your sources didn't tell you?" He looked at each of us in turn. "Your sources didn't tell you shit. This has all been a bluff." The shotgun rose from its place at his side.

"We've already told our lawyer about you. He's in Chicago. You won't be able to kill him. He's not stuck in the middle of godforsaken nowhere."

"But I could still kill you."

"Oh, give it a rest, you moron. You can no more kill us than flap your arms and fly to the moon. Your stupid shotgun is a poor prop for a sick ego. You're much better scaring lonely and frightened people in the middle of the night. How's this? You're life is going to be in ruins unless you open up to us right now."

"I'd at least have the pleasure of killing you. I'd be willing to take my chances with a jury down here."

The expedient thing seemed to be to whack him one and grab the shotgun. So I did. The scuffle was brief. I wasn't sure whether he didn't expect an attack from a fairy, or he was just a fat old blowhard. Either way, now I had the gun.

I opened the breech and dropped the shells into my hand. I threw the gun out the screen door into the rain.

"So did you and your buddies get together and kill the sheriff, or were you desperate enough to do it yourself?"

"I didn't kill him and I don't know who did. I had nothing to do with it. Far as I know, neither did any of my friends."

"Where were you the night the sheriff was murdered?"

"We had a Klan meeting. I have witnesses to where I was. A friend dropped me off here at the house around three in the morning. I went to bed."

"You want to tell us who your witnesses are?"

He looked at Scott and laughed. "Why don't you go talk to your brother Hiram?"

"What?"

Holcomb laughed. "It may or may not come to my word against yours about having a black mistress, but you'll have to talk to your own family, Carpenter."

"Hiram would never hurt anybody," Scott said. "He was at the hospital that night."

Holcomb laughed again. "Not after midnight. Lot of hate in the Carpenter family. You folks have tried to lord it over everybody. The poor family struggling for years, but acting like they're better than everybody else. Then huge pots of money because one kid is lucky enough to be a gifted athlete. I can't stand any of you. But look to your own for real hatred."

"My brother would never hurt me or anyone I know. He

172

wouldn't plot against me or someone I loved." Scott was pale and trembling. Knowing that his brother was in the Klan and probably actively working against him shouldn't have been a surprise. I didn't bother to point out to him that Hiram had written us the vicious letter and that he was probably the one who helped keep Shannon and Nathan against us. It didn't seem the right time for "I told you so."

Holcomb said, "Take your threats, my shotgun if you want, and go. Talk to your own family."

He wouldn't answer any more questions even under threat. He knew he'd hit home with Scott about his brother.

When we walked out the door, Violet's car was at the curb. I picked up the shotgun, and we hurried ourselves inside. Scott sat in front next to Violet.

"Didn't see you at the library," she said. "Thought I'd check here. What happened?"

Scott told her.

I placed the shotgun on the floor of the car. I was uncomfortable in the ill-fitting clothes. I wasn't soaked, but water seemed to be seeping into my pores.

"That's not true about Hiram," Scott said. "Holcomb is just trying to protect himself. No brother of mine would do such a thing."

"I haven't been able to get hold of Hiram," Violet said. "I was down at the library. We decided to move everything. We had over a hundred volunteers. We even trucked part of the collection to the next county. It's started to rain an inch an hour. Now the weather bureau isn't sure when it's going to stop. Water is rising fast."

"Should we evacuate Daddy?" Scott asked.

"We should stop at the hospital anyway," I said. "Maybe Hiram will be there."

"He didn't do anything," Scott said. "He'd never do

something to hurt me. I'm his flesh and blood. I know him. He wouldn't."

"I'm going to talk to him," I said. "I know you love him, but when is the last time that you really talked to him? Years ago. You don't know him anymore. You're adults now, and his world has been different from yours for many years."

"He wouldn't do anything to hurt me," Scott insisted.

I kept silent as Violet drove us to the other side of town and the hospital. On the second floor, Scott called in to the CCU. Shannon and Nathan came out and Scott went in.

In the waiting room his brother and sister clustered as far as they could away from Violet and me. Violet had confirmed that a few weeks ago Shannon had quit her job as a secretary for a local funeral parlor on the town square. I wondered if that had anything to do with Jasper saying she'd been acting odd. Shannon wore a long dress and a silk blouse with sleeves down to her wrists and buttons clasped shut to the neck. Nathan wore a sport coat, tie, and faded blue jeans. They glared at me as I walked over and asked who was supposed to relieve them. They said it was Hiram; he'd be there in half an hour. Their cousin Sally was the other Carpenter on duty in their father's room.

Violet and I walked up to the third floor and visited Dennis. We only got a glance in the room. He was asleep. Large swaths of bandages covered his face. It was long after regular visiting hours were over. A nurse walked by and gently moved us away. She told us he was doing okay, and they were fairly certain he would not lose his eye.

Back on the second floor, Nathan and Shannon had left. While waiting for Hiram, I said to Violet, "One thing I don't get about this town. If they've got all these secrets and everybody knows everybody else's business, then how come everybody didn't know all this information about the sheriff?"

174

"Sometimes you know things and you shut your eyes. Or maybe it's that lots of people know cheap, tawdry gossip, but not really awful secrets. You can know Uncle Felix's great-aunt drank whiskey from a slop pail during the full moon, but it's not really vital, cheap, tawdry gossip. Genealogy, background, and pettiness don't add up to practical knowledge."

"I think I understand."

"Speaking of cheap, tawdry gossip, I can't believe Magnolia is really boffing Al Holcomb. I can't believe he wouldn't be scared about people finding out. His Klan buddies would go nuts."

"Maybe old Al pushed one of his buddies over the edge. Maybe others had grudges against Peter Woodall. Al just encouraged them. Lit the spark."

"Could be. But if Hiram hates Scott, why kill the sheriff? You've got Jasper saying Hiram was doing something illegal, but you've got no proof. Sticking the body in the car could just have easily gotten Scott under suspicion, and why take a chance being seen? So, say all the sheriff wanted was political support. It's blackmail, but it's not the end of the world. You have to support somebody in an election."

"People's emotions get involved," I said. "It could be an election for dogcatcher, but if people are angry or desperate, you never know what could happen. I think the other major motivation for murder would be the sheriff getting his jollies from women he threatened to lock up."

"I can see a southern gentleman defending his own and his wife's honor. Maybe the sheriff got hold of Hiram's wife."

"I intend to ask Hiram a lot of questions, and I want to do it without Scott around."

Hiram walked in forty-five minutes later. He entered the lounge, saw us, and hesitated.

"I need to talk to you," I said.

He turned to leave.

Violet glided to the door and blocked his exit.

I stood up.

"I'm going to talk to you, Hiram. We know you're in the Klan."

"Violet, you get out of my way. I'm not going to hurt a lady, but you move out of my way or I'll *put* you out of my way."

"No," I said. "You're done putting anybody anywhere. Or is that what you did with the sheriff?"

He reached for Violet.

In a flash his hand and arm were twisted up against his back.

"What are you looking so stunned about?" Violet said to me. "You think I can't protect myself?"

"I'm impressed," I said.

Hiram struggled.

Violet wrenched his hand higher and tighter.

"Ouch! Leggo!"

"Stop moving around," Violet ordered.

He held still.

"That old stereotype of the southern woman as soft and pliable and barefoot and pregnant and staying home and slopping the hogs is dead. We can take care of ourselves. You listen to Tom. You talk to him."

"Figures a faggot has to have a woman protect him."

"Hiram," I said. "Why don't you *all* just shut up and listen for *all* of a few minutes and you *all* can give us answers so we *all* can find out who *all* killed the sheriff and then I *all* can get out of you *all*'s town?"

An elderly couple appeared in the doorway. Arm in arm, they supported each other. They gave us quizzical looks. Violet moved Hiram out of their way. The woman called into the CCU. She hung up and told her companion it would be a few minutes before they could go in.

Hiram did not beg them to call for help. He struggled briefly, but complied with our request that we change our venue. We moved down the hall to the conference room where Dr. McLarty had talked to the family. Violet marched him into the room, let Hiram go, and said, "I'll be outside the door if you need me."

"Thanks," I said.

I stood between Hiram and the door. He wore black jeans and a black T-shirt and was sitting on the edge of a backless couch. He rubbed his hands together. "What?" he growled.

"I know you hate me," I said. "But why hate Scott? He's your brother. He doesn't think you'd ever do anything to hurt him."

"I don't have to talk to you. Violet's not here to beat me up."

"What is it with you? Do we need to mud-wrestle at midnight in a swamp? Beat each other up? Duel at fifty paces with sawed-off shotguns? You don't get to hide behind bullying nonanswers. You're in the Klan. I want to know where you went after your dad's operation, the night the sheriff was killed. Jasper Williams told me you were doing something illegal on your farm, although he didn't know what. We are going to have a little talk. If necessary, we're going to have state and federal investigators down here. Our lawyer is already working on that. We aren't going to trust to the local authorities. Maybe they'll protect you some, but when the feds get down here, they're going to want real answers. Because you're Scott's brother, I'd do some to try and protect you for his sake, but now I want some answers. Quiet and civilized or angry and rude, whichever way you prefer."

He began smacking one fist into the open palm of the other.

"How come you're a member of the Klan?"

"I want to be."

"Why don't you elaborate for me?"

The fist moved faster. He said, "I believe in what they stand for. Racial purity. Superiority of whites. Keeping the godless out. Keepin' faggots like you in your place."

"Don't you love Scott?"

He laughed but didn't smile. "I've hated him since we were kids. He always got everything. I was always compared to him by everybody."

"That wasn't his fault."

"Nothing was ever Scott's fault! He never paid attention to anyone besides himself. The whole family figured he was our ticket out of this swamp. Well, I busted my ass. I got out of the swamp on my own. I may not be as rich as my brother, but I've got no reason to hang my head."

"Was there a Klan meeting the night the sheriff was killed?"

"Yes. I drove Al to his place and then went home to bed. No, I don't have a witness, but I didn't kill the sheriff."

"What did Peter Woodall catch you doing on your farm that was illegal?"

"Nothing."

"Jasper didn't think you were growing illegal drugs. I think he would have been able to tell that. What was it?"

"Nothing."

"Have to get the federal marshals down there to see what this is all about. That's the nice thing about Scott having tons of money. The rich are treated differently. We'll have this place crawling with agents soon."

"Let 'em crawl." He stood up. "See, I didn't kill the sheriff. No witnesses. No guilt. And I'm not going to have to put up with you for long. Good-bye."

He strode toward the door.

I grabbed his arm to stop him. "What do you mean,

you're not going to have to put up with me?"

He laughed, then shoved me hard.

I kept my grip on his arm and twisted it behind his back.

He bellowed and squirmed. Violet threw open the door. Scott and Cody stood behind her. They saw me bending Hiram's arm behind his back.

"Let him go," Scott said.

Hiram wrenched himself away, straightened himself up, glared at all of us, walked into the hall, and turned around.

The four of them looked at me.

I said, "He says he didn't kill the sheriff."

Cody said, "You're under arrest."

10

Hiram grinned. I began a protest. Scott looked furious. Cody simply twisted his head to the radio attached to his shoulder and said, "He's here. I need backup to take him in."

Scott said to me, "Hiram wouldn't kill anybody." To Cody he said, "You can't arrest Tom. He didn't kill anybody."

Cody repeated, "You're under arrest."

His backup arrived moments later. I didn't struggle. Cody pulled handcuffs off the belt that surrounded his narrow hips. I wanted to throttle him. He was impervious to any questions we tried to ask. He patted me down for weapons, and I wound up with my hands cuffed behind my back, being hustled downstairs.

At the exit Scott tried to hug me, but they yanked me away. Three cop cars waited in the parking lot. Two cops and I crossed the few feet between car and overhang through the rain. They opened the car door for me and I stooped down. Cody put his hand on top of my head so I wouldn't bang it against the roof.

Scott called, "I'll get you out."

The door slammed and I was inside. I looked back and saw Violet rushing across the parking lot toward her car.

I saw Scott waving his finger in his brother's face. He seemed to be angrily berating him, but I couldn't make out the words.

Cody and an older cop I didn't recognize sat in the front. I asked questions through the screen. The older cop told me to shut up. I did. I watched as Violet's car pulled out behind us and followed.

If I'd known any of the lyrics to "Marching Through Georgia," I'd have sung them. If I'd known even the tune, I'd have hummed it. And probably would have been shot on the spot.

Minutes later they led me into the lynching emporium they called a jail.

The interior of the jail smelled of damp and mold, excrement and urine. No air-conditioning. The tiny slits that served as windows in the first room we entered were all open. I heard the rain rushing off the roof. Strips of masking tape above the desk stayed absolutely still. Not the slightest breeze. The tape was covered with black specks—ersatz flypaper.

"I get a phone call," I said.

"No calls."

They brought me across a five-foot entryway to a large counter that stretched nine-tenths of the way across the room, blocking the way into the back. The last tenth was on the right: a barred doorway.

A white woman with her gray hair tied back in a bun pulled out a large manila envelope from the top drawer of the desk she was sitting at. She didn't wear a uniform. She brought the envelope to the counter and said, "Put his belongings in here."

They took my wallet, change, car keys, handkerchief, watch, and pen and placed them in the bag. Then they undid my belt, pulled it out, and shoved it in the envelope. Cody untied my shoelaces and placed them in the receptacle. On a sheet of paper the woman listed everything they placed inside. She opened my wallet and inventoried the contents on a different sheet of paper. When she was finished, she sealed the envelope and tossed it on top of a desk behind her.

"Do I get to know the charge?" I asked quietly.

Nobody answered.

"No calls? No charge? I want my lawyer."

They didn't yell, scream, or carry on. They mumbled a few simple commands but said nothing else. This frightened me.

My shoes flapped on my feet as they led me through the barred doorway. The area behind the counter had three desks filled with the knickknacks, pictures of kids, and piles of papers you'd expect on a bureaucrat's desk. The door we met was solid steel, with a three-by-five-inch sliding panel in it.

Cody pressed a buzzer on the right. The panel slid open and two eyes looked out, moved from left to right, and disappeared. The panel closed and seconds later the door swung open. A step or two farther, a creak of a hinge as the door shut, and I was in. To the left was a desk with a lamp and an open newspaper spread out on top of it. An older African-American cop pulled out a large ring filled with keys. He selected a small silver one and unlocked another metal door, this one without a peephole.

The cops exchanged minimal greetings, but I was not discussed in the least. It was as if I was expected, and they all knew their roles. I felt like an actor who'd walked into the wrong play.

I didn't try to yell, shout, scream, or fight. They had the upper hand. I knew it. They knew it. At this moment, fighting was useless.

The next room was long and rectangular, and I guessed it must stretch the rest of the length of the jail. On the right where we stood, it was a broad hallway, eight feet across. The cells were on the left. We walked past eight empty ones before coming to a ninth. The old cop selected another key, unlocked the door, and swung it open. They unlocked the handcuffs. Cody placed a hand on my shoulder and directed me inside.

No one had been violent. No one had been cruel. No one had yelled or tried to intimidate me. They had treated me like a thing, and that scared me.

They left.

Riveted to the wall of the cell was an iron toilet with no seat. The bed had a frame bolted to the floor. I looked under the eighth-inch-thick mattress. The slats were welded to the frame.

I looked back the way I'd come. Nobody. There was one more cell in the row. Lack of X-ray vision prevented me from seeing through the gray cinderblock walls into the cells on either side.

"Anybody there?" I called.

Silence.

None of the cells I'd seen had windows. Dim illumination shown from a fluorescent light over the door at the far end. Did they turn on more lights in the morning, or was it always eternally gloomy in here?

I could hear the rain on the roof and nothing else. I lay back on the mattress. First, I decided to give my situation a good solid worry. Then I opted for a healthy bout of self-pity. If you can't feel sorry for yourself, who's going to do it for you? And frankly, who but yourself is better at feeling sorry for yourself?

Then I worried about Scott and his dad. I knew Scott would be doing everything he could to get me out of here. I hoped for a visit from Beauregard Lee, the lawyer from Atlanta, or any other form of rescue. They'd have to give me some kind of hearing eventually. Scott, lawyers, press, somebody would be able to help me. I hoped Violet was outside now, doing what she could—although I doubted if all her southern charms would be enough to huff and puff and blow this house of bricks down.

The heat was miserable. Damp clung to every inch of my body. I'd been in the middle of pouring rain and putrid humidity so long by now, I felt like I'd been immersed in a pool of peppered water. I couldn't see any visible vermin on the mattress, but I didn't take my clothes off to lie down. There was no pillow. I lay and sweated, then sweated some more. I tried standing. Gave pacing a shot. Took a whirl on bellowing angrily at the top of my lungs. The light stayed on, the rain fell, and nobody responded.

Angry thoughts mixed with helplessness and rage as I lay back down. I tried thinking of all the nastiest tortures I would like to inflict on the dumber denizens of Brinard County. Finally, I fell asleep to the falling of the rain.

I woke up to thunder some time later. I listened to it and felt somehow comforted. They could try and do any number of things to me, but nature would be stronger than any of us. I don't know why this soothed me, but it did. I fell back to sleep almost immediately.

At first I couldn't tell what woke me next. I blinked at the ceiling. The amount of light was the same. The cracks and lines hadn't altered. I realized two things. First, the rain had stopped, or was falling too lightly to register on the roof. The second was more ominous. The place stunk worse than it had. I looked down. Water swirled on the floor. It had risen about two inches on the frame.

I stood on the bed. "Hey!" I shouted. I couldn't see where the water was coming from, but it was brown and unhealthy-looking. I bellowed loudly and angrily and continuously until my throat was raw. After I exhausted this useless option, I checked the water again. Four inches up the frame. I banged my hands on the wall and ceiling.

I heard a brief *phfft,* a sizzle, and the lights winked out. Total darkness.

A couple of thoughts struck me. They were trying to drown me, and turning out the lights was extra torture. What made me hesitate in this conclusion was that the lights hadn't gone out as if someone was shutting them off. Plus, how could they flood ten feet of room floor-to-ceiling? Maybe I wasn't being killed deliberately. Maybe I was being totally forgotten.

A major panic seemed in order. I know I'm an ex-Marine, and I like to think I'm tough, but although it certainly isn't macho, I was scared witless. I'm not proud of what I did for the next few minutes, but I'm not ashamed, either. It just happened.

For an unknown amount of time, I lost all sense of proportion and my own humanity. Hammering until my fists were bloody and screaming on tortured vocal cords, I let loose with every ounce of rage in my body.

No response.

I knelt on the bed frame and drew deep breaths. I must have crouched there for some time or the water was rising swiftly, because dampness on my knees startled me. Rationality slowly returned.

I stepped into the water. It came to just below my knees. I couldn't think about the filth I was walking in. In the dark I felt behind me for the bed. Methodically I yanked at the frame and the slats. Stuck solid to wall and floor. Putting my hands in front of me, I moved to the bars, and on each one in turn I twisted, pounded, pulled, slapped, and yanked, but they moved not an inch. Darkness totally surrounded me. Not an outlet or way of saving myself came to mind.

I shouted again.

I thought I heard a response.

I bellowed louder.

Definitely voices responding. I thought I heard the creak of a door hinge. Dim light entered the room.

"Tom?" a voice called.

"Violet?" I couldn't see to the doorway, but I thought I recognized her voice.

"Tom!"

"Get me out of here!" I yelled. I could see the water eddy and swirl. Pockets of filth spun by.

I heard sloshing. Cody came into view. He was holding on to Violet, who had a rope tied around her waist.

"I told you he was in here," Violet said.

Cody said, "Wainwright Richardson told me you'd been moved. We've got to hurry."

Violet wore hip-wader boots and a jacket zipped to her throat. Her hair was soaked.

"Thank you for coming," I said.

Cody wore unbuckled knee-high boots. His pants were soaked to the crotch. A red-and-yellow-striped emergency jacket covered his uniform shirt. He fumbled with the key ring. Tried four different ones before the lock clicked.

"Hang on to Violet," he said. "If the building goes while we're in here, just hold on."

He grabbed the rope and began walking hand over hand back the way they had come. I clutched the rope tightly and imitated his gestures. Violet came behind.

The doors to the front were open and I could see gray outdoor light. Chunks of raw sewage drifted by my legs in the water, which was now halfway up my thigh.

In the doorway I saw a boat with men in the same red-and-yellow-striped jackets as Cody. One of them had the other end of the rope tied around him while another held the throttle for the motor of the boat.

"Hurry!" a man in his fifties called. The building seemed to tilt around me.

Cody splashed through the counter door. I heard the

building groan. The three of us pulled ourselves through the vile fluid.

Out the front door, I looked back for Violet.

"Go!" she ordered.

In the water outside, I could feel my feet beginning to be swept away by the torrent. The current sucked away my laceless shoes.

I clutched at the rope. Hands grabbed me and lifted me into the boat.

Cody, Violet, and I sat in the middle of a twelve-foot craft. As soon as we were in, the motor roared louder, and we pulled away from the building.

The jail slowly turned sideways, drifted in the current for a minute, collapsed on itself, and then was swept away.

I felt occasional raindrops on my head.

I looked around. The water was at the base of the court-house. A cop car was covered by water up to its Mars lights. The water had reached the first-floor windows of the police station. I gazed back at the river itself as the boat neared the new bank. I saw swing sets, yard furniture, tires, and tree limbs swish past in the mud-dark water. The creek was at least fifty feet across by now. In one of the deeper parts the top of a truck was sweeping by, along with logs, branches, and whole trees, revolving and dipping in the flood.

We arrived ten feet from Della's Bar-b-que, stepped out of the boat into water up to our knees, and were pulled to dry land by a number of hands.

Forty or fifty people stood on the bank. Four or five of them had video cameras recording the destruction.

"Thank you again," I said to Violet and Cody.

He shrugged.

A kid about ten rushed up to me with a pair of knee-high boots. He clutched three other pairs in his left hand. "Here, mister," he said. "We got these for everybody."

I thanked him. He dashed off to his next person.

Violet said. "You probably saw me follow you. They refused to answer any of my questions. I went back and forth between the police station, the jail, and the hospital for hours. Scott and I placed about a million calls last night. So did your lawyer in Chicago and the one in Atlanta. It was impossible to get you out in the middle of the night. We couldn't even get an answer about why they arrested you."

We inched back from the edge as the water continued to rise.

Violet continued. "When I came back this time, there was no one in the jail and the keys were gone. The water was up to the doorway. I ran to the police station, but no one would listen. I finally found Cody and made him look."

"Am I still under arrest?" I asked her.

"I don't know. I didn't ask."

We turned to Cody.

Violet put her hand on his arm. "Richardson wanted him dead, and you know it. That's murder."

"Maybe he thought someone moved him."

"Do you believe that?"

He shrugged.

A truck pulling a boat turned into the square from the dry end. It halted several feet from us and turned so that the boat slowly entered the water. One of the emergency workers in the cab yelled, "Come on, Cody! This is the last boat to be found. We've got to move on those folks north of town in the trailer park!"

Cody hesitated, looked around for assistance.

Violet said, "He can't go anywhere. The town's cut off. He can help load sandbags at the hospital. You know Richardson tried to kill him. Tom didn't hurt anyone."

"Let's move, Cody! People are hurtin' real bad."

"We'll get answers to these questions later," Cody said, and hurried off.

A large snake slithered out of the water. One of the people standing near the edge grabbed a sandbag from a small pile and crushed the animal.

"Why aren't they building a levee?" I asked.

"Not enough sandbags in the county," Violet said. "They've never had a flood like this. Highest the water ever got before was up to the jail back last century. They're keeping the sandbags to try and save the water treatment plant and the hospital and a few other places."

"Can they evacuate Scott's father?"

"The town's cut off. Help can't get in or out. The roads are completely flooded. They have an emergency helicopter from Macon. Don't know how soon it could get here. When the storm lets up some more, it'll be used for rescuing stranded people. No place can send more help. It's awful for miles around."

"Can we still get to the hospital?"

No one challenged my walking away, getting into Violet's car, and driving off down the road.

"Rain seems to have let up," I said.

"We've had at least fifteen inches. If it hadn't been so dry in the first place, we'd probably all have floated away already. They evacuated as many people in town as they could overnight."

"How long was I in jail?"

"About six hours. Water came faster than anybody imagined."

"Will it overrun the whole town?"

"I hope not."

About three hundred people clustered in the hospital parking lot. I saw Hiram, Shannon, Nathan, and Mary, along with Clara Thorton, Wainwright Richardson, and Al Holcomb.

Inside the hospital the lights were dim but still working. We took the stairs up. The air-conditioning was off, but the hospital was not yet uncomfortable.

Scott was in the hall with his mom.

He hurried to me. "You smell awful," he said. He embraced me tightly. "How'd you get out?"

I told him the story of my incarceration and rescue. When I finished, I got another fierce hug. Then he asked, "Are you still under arrest?"

"Everybody's too busy with the flood to notice me right now. How's your dad? Are they going to move him?"

"The emergency generator can hold out for several days. They don't want to move him if they don't have to."

I looked at his mother. "Can you get back to the farm?"

Scott said, "We don't know if the road is still open or not. I made it last night and I got you a change of clothes. The farm is on a rise in the forest, and there's only a little fishing crick at the far end of the place."

Violet said, "I'm not sure they could spare anybody to try and make it back to the farm now. And if something went wrong and she had to evacuate, help would be too far away."

"I'm going to make sure there's space here," Scott said. "I don't want her in some shelter if I can help it."

"We may all be in one before this is over," Violet said.

"I'll be fine," Mrs. Carpenter said.

A woman came around a corner and hurried toward us. Her name badge identified her as a hospital administrator. She said, "They're starting to sandbag on the west side of the hospital. We need all the help we can get."

Mrs. Carpenter said she could take care of herself and her husband. I changed into the clothes Scott had brought me, and Violet, Scott, and I hurried down the stairs.

The west side of the hospital was the farthest away from where I'd found the sheriff's body. Bags, sand, earth-moving equipment, and hundreds of people worked purposefully. In the middle of a group of men stood Clara Thorton, making decisions and giving orders.

Because of his groin injury, Scott was assigned to the less strenuous jobs.

The creek ran along a small parkway on this side. All the houses and businesses on the far side of the creek were under water. Because of the slope, the water had been forced away from the hospital. Now, however, the water was rising toward us. The barrier we had to create was at least four hundred feet long. I joined a line of people passing sandbags to the new levee.

All of us worked with the mindless enthusiasm of those with a purpose and a chance to be heroic. We might be saving a few buildings in an insignificant town, but these were people's homes, the hospital, and the businesses that people lived in, worked in, and cared about.

At noon, word passed among the workers that the water filtration plant was safe for now. As a precaution some were given duty to fill every possible container with water. No one could predict if the water plant would last, and every drop was precious.

At one, word spread that the ten-foot levee we were building wasn't enough; another five feet were necessary, if not more. Weariness gave way to total aching and beyond. You wanted to take a break, but it was impossible. Someone had thought to salvage all the bottled water and soft drinks from the grocery store before it was inundated. We drank sparingly.

At two, the rain stopped altogether. By two-thirty the sky was bright blue. People cheered the first rays of the sun. By four o'clock we wished for any kind of cover from the painful brightness. The heat rose and the stench increased.

At one point I found myself on top of the levee. They'd had to extend it on both ends by two hundred feet. Slowly the ends had begun to turn on themselves. Eventually I thought we might totally encircle the hospital. There was a ten-foot ridge running several hundred feet along the east side of the hospital. Each end could meet that if we had to. If the water overtopped the ridge, we were all going to have to be rescued by boats.

I flung down sandbags upon sandbags. The water was six feet below where I was standing. I looked out over the rushing water.

Up and down the line people were stopping and staring, and I followed their gaze. I saw a man sitting in a tree, holding a German shepherd in his arms. We watched the drama unfold. The water was three feet from his legs. Firefighters on a hook-and-ladder truck were trying to reach him.

The fire truck was on a slight rise in the front yard of the last house about to be inundated, about two hundred feet from the far right of the levee. The way out was still clear of water. They extended the ladder as far as it would go. It was five feet short of the man. The water was still rising rapidly, so the truck could go no farther into the water, and would have to move back itself if it and its rescuers couldn't save him in the next few minutes.

I saw men speaking into portable phones and walkie-talkies. I assumed any boats nearby were already in use making other rescues. None appeared on the horizon. If the man was going to be saved, this was his last chance.

The fireman at the far end of the ladder threw him a rope. The man in the tree tied the end around his dog and shoved the animal into the water. The man stepped farther up into the tree. The branches swayed. He could go no higher up. The firemen pulled the dog to safety.

Again the rope was thrown. It fell short. The water reached the front wheels of the fire truck. A third time and the man caught the end of the rope. He tied it around his waist and hung on to the end. The fire truck pulled away, taking man and beast with them out of harm's way.

We cheered and returned to work.

At six o'clock, as they had at noon, people gave out sandwiches and cans of pop. We could drink half the can and were given a plastic cup with which to share our bounty with a neighbor. For this feast I found myself next to an African-American woman in her early twenties. We smiled at each other as we savored our food and brief respite.

I bumped into Shannon and Hiram Carpenter about half an hour after this. He aimed a nearly full sandbag at my foot. I yanked it out of the way. Shannon sneered. Hiram glared at me, muttered "Fuck you," and walked away.

All that day none of the other workers had chosen to respond, positively or negatively, to my presence. Plenty of time for hate after the flood.

By the time night fell, one road still led out of the parking lot and connected us to the rest of the town. A report came that five feet of water was swirling through the courthouse. A helicopter flew over.

We had a snake, alligator, and verminous critter patrol set up. Sightings had been made of all of the above. Plus there was a fear of rabid animals.

The water still rose, but at a slower rate. Three shifts of workers were set up to alternate work during the night.

Scott and I stood on the top of the levee and watched the full moon rise. The dark turned to soft gray, and silvery patterns flickered on the water. Stars shone brightly and reflected in the surface of the rushing torrent.

"Is the farm okay?"

"I don't know. I'd hate to see the house gone. We should be okay, but I'm not sure about Nathan's and Hiram's places. I haven't seen them to talk to them."

"How is Violet?"

"I think she left just before sunset to check on the library. The books should be safe. She was concerned about the building itself."

"What did the lawyers say last night when you and Violet called them?"

"Todd had it all lined up to get tons of media coverage down here. Some of the networks, the *New York Times,* the *Washington Post,* and he didn't know who all else, were on their way. I'm sure they're covering the flood now."

"And they have no way of getting into town anyway. Outside help isn't going to be concerned about saving my butt while most of the countryside is trying to float to the Gulf."

While Scott went to look in on his mom and dad, I tried to locate Cody to check on my official status. I couldn't find any officials to talk to. The boots I had been given were clunky and uncomfortable, but every bone in my body hurt, so sore feet were hardly noticeable.

Violet found me at the entrance to the hospital.

"Library okay?" I asked.

"Water's at least seven feet deep. Building is probably ruined. Thank God the books, computers, and files are safe."

Hospital workers passed out blankets for those of us sleeping on the floor in the hallway or outside. Most everybody chose to sleep under the stars. The halls had begun to smell of sweat and lack of deodorant. Outdoors we had the smell of flood, but the air wasn't as close. A group of nine- and ten-year-olds walked around with spray cans of mosquito repellent.

Scott reported that his father rested peacefully. His mother was napping on a couch upstairs with his sisters on guard. He hadn't seen his brothers.

Violet, Scott, and I found a patch of ground to sleep on. All the cars in the parking lot were filled with kids bedded down on front and backseats. Trunks were open with in-

ain. We'd all have to cram road was still open to the was already filled to capac-

ification, all lost in the de-

lot gave not an inch in my le position and fall asleep. scing. I'd thought of making hen I thought I'd better grow up a to them talk softly of warm nights like these in summer long past, of whispered secrets that now seemed remote and comfortable. They spoke of teenage tragedies, couples who broke up, people they wish they still knew, people they were glad they hadn't seen in years and hoped never to see again.

The moon was almost directly overhead. The gray light was enough to show one crew working at the far end of the levee closest to the ridge. Another team was filling sandbags near the center where we had started that morning. Watchers walked the top of the levee.

I lay on my back and gazed at the stars. Scott and Violet talked about the time they were king and queen of the senior prom.

"I was so proud to walk down the center of the gym with you," Scott said. "I was just terrified that you'd expect something later."

Violet laughed. "You don't know how desperately I wanted something later."

They both chuckled.

Someone shouted from the far side of the parking lot. In seconds people were up and running toward the levee. Water rushed through a three-foot gap in the dike. Every second it grew wider. People raced to help. Lines formed quickly. Sandbags flew. I found myself between a hunky teenager and a woman in her fifties with enormous breasts and huge arms. They handed us sandbags from our right, and from our left water poured onto us. The woman, the teenager, and I competed with at least forty other hands slinging bags of sand into the breech. Water sluiced around us.

Someone shouted, "Move back, it's going to go! Run!"

I whirled my head around. No one around me retreated. The water was up to my waist. People on top of the dike hurled sandbags from the sides. Twenty of us were right at the opening. I turned for another bag and something bumped into my left hand.

When I looked down I saw moonlight glittering on the bloated, no longer handsome face of Jasper Williams.

I called out, but my shout was lost in the uproar of desperate humans and rushing water. The huge woman and the teenager saw him. We paused for a second. The woman grabbed his hand for an instant.

"He's dead," she said.

Sandbags continued to rain down from above. The corpse wedged into the opening and provided an excellent break to a ton of water.

The kid yelled, "We can get him later!"

The woman nodded. She shouted, "He hurt people when he was alive, maybe he'll save a few now!"

We piled sandbags around and on top of him. In seconds his body was completely covered. Minutes later the water from the break was down to a trickle, and finally it stopped.

The woman said, "I want to get hold of the dim-bulb dumb shit who yelled 'Run!'"

The kid said, "It was that asshole Al Holcomb."

I enjoyed the idea of him being the goat of the town.

The woman and the kid promised to find someone to report the dead body to. I was just pleased that Jasper was really dead.

I found Scott on top of the levee helping reinforce another spot that looked weak. I figured he'd aggravate his injury, but there wasn't time to worry about that now. I lent a hand. When I stopped my work for the night, the moon was on the western horizon. Full dawn wasn't far off.

Scott limped slightly as he and I wandered back to the hospital, climbed the stairs, and found his mom.

She was awake. She had insisted that Shannon and Mary go out to help with repairing the dike. Scott and his mom went in to look at his dad.

I sat on the couch and felt more tired than I had ever been in my life. Dr. McLarty poked his head in the door of the lounge. He wore jeans, boots, and a green T-shirt with "Burr County General Hospital" stenciled on the front. His clothes were as wet as anyone's I'd seen that day.

"You okay?" he asked.

"Yeah. You out at the flood?"

"Just finished filling my millionth sandbag. They say the crest will be late this afternoon. The river isn't rising as rapidly. We might make it."

He sat down. "I talked to some people," he said. "They think they might know some things to help you."

"Who?"

"Two lesbians. Are you still in danger?"

"I think I'm still arrested. As soon as the sky stops falling, I'm afraid I'll be back in the tender hands of Burr

County." I gave him a brief summary of what had happened at the jail. When I finished, he led me to a third-floor room near Dennis's.

He told me Dennis would be able to leave the hospital in a day or two. "You should both be happy to be alive. I don't know if plastic surgery can repair what Jasper destroyed."

I told him about the corpse.

"Good. The town bully is dead."

We entered an unoccupied doctor's office. Sitting in one chair was a grossly overweight woman of about twenty-five. Next to her and holding her hand was a woman in her early forties. She might have been a university professor, except, like the rest of us, her clothes were damp and she smelled like she'd been dipped in shit. She wore gold-rimmed glasses and had a quiet demeanor, holding herself properly, shoulders back.

McLarty introduced them as Sylvia and Janis.

Sylvia, the professorish one, said, "I own a shop on Main Street on the square. I managed to move most of my inventory. I make dresses."

Janis said, "I'm part-owner of the Dixie Square Beauty Shop." I couldn't imagine her being much of an advertisement for her own products, but if they were willing to help, I was ready to pass out sainthoods and buy every article they sold in their stores—maybe even fly in for haircuts once a month. Whatever it took.

Janis said, "Dr. McLarty urged us to help you. We're a little uncertain. We have to live in this town."

"I promise I won't bring your names into any of this."

The women looked at each other, then over to McLarty.

Sylvia said, "We have to be very careful. We're the only two lesbians in the area who own shops, and we aren't out in the open. If word got around, the least that would happen is our store windows would be broken. If there is anything left to break after this disaster."

Again I promised to keep them out of it.

Janis said, "We have a small women's group from the surrounding counties."

"Magnolia, from the bar, mentioned one," I said.

"Yes, we're a subgroup. It's very informal. Magnolia is so tough and nothing seems to scare her."

"Is she a lesbian?"

"She says she's open-minded," Janis said. "Some nights she prefers one, some the other, mostly none."

"What's important," Sylvia said, "is that we know something was supposed to happen this week. We aren't sure what."

"Who was planning to act?"

"Those women whom the sheriff had victimized. Some of them told. Word got back to the Klan. Supposedly they were going to try and organize something at their meeting."

"Didn't the noble male giving his all for the honor of southern womanhood go out with *Gone with the Wind?*"

"No," Janis said.

Sylvia said, "What the sheriff was doing was despicable."

"Why not go to the police?" I asked, and realized instantly it wasn't the brightest question. Then I asked about other jurisdictions, other judges and lawyers.

"A woman would have to prove it. There was no physical proof, no evidence."

"Who were the women and men involved?" I asked.

"We only know some of them," Janis said. "And at least one was in the Klan, so he could ask for them to take action."

"Who were they?" I asked.

"There are three. Jennifer Essex, the wife of Harvey Essex, one of the policemen on the force."

"Young blond fella. I saw him questioning you the morning of the murder," McLarty said.

"Betty Dixon told her brother Chad. She's only eighteen and not married."

They hesitated.

"Who's the third?" McLarty asked.

"Shannon Carpenter. Hiram was probably the one who was going to bring it to the Klan for action."

They knew only those names and that something was supposed to happen. They knew no more and didn't want to prolong the interview. They seemed to want to run as fast as they could in the other direction. After exacting another promise from me not to say anything about them, they left.

I decided it would not be helpful to tell Scott about this latest revelation. I was dismayed but not surprised that his family was in this deeply.

I left the hospital. In the parking lot, the assigned crews were continuing to fill sandbags and stack them at key points. Many people were lined up at Red Cross coffee machines. The sun was already beginning to warm the fetid air.

I searched the crowd for any of the people mentioned.

11

I saw Clara Thorton holding a small child in her arms. She spotted me, delivered the youth to another woman, and walked over.

"Thank you for your help," she said.

"I did what everyone else was doing."

"You didn't have to. This isn't your town. I appreciate it. I don't pretend to understand you. I'm still uncomfortable about all this, but you deserve some help. I heard you were arrested."

"Yes. Am I still?"

"Not as far as I'm concerned, but that's not my department. Nor do I know why you were arrested. I do know that you were taken at the direct order of Wainwright Richardson. I believe you were deliberately left in the jail to die. Wainwright is another one who was working against me. It took me some time since noon yesterday to find this out, and I had to apply a great deal of pressure, but I can say with reasonable certainty that Wainwright was Jasper Williams's contact in the hierarchy of county government. Wainwright supports many of Jasper's causes. I don't know more. Your problem is that Wainwright is in charge of law enforcement. When he gets a minute, you will be arrested again, unless you get some high-powered lawyers or federal marshals down here. I cannot protect you there. The police will probably listen to Wainwright."

I hoped at least Cody would see the light.

It felt like I was trying to avoid half the town while I hunted for the other half to question. First, I searched in the direction of the levee. I wanted to find Harvey, Shannon and Hiram Carpenter, and Wainwright Richardson when he wasn't surrounded by a gaggle of cops. I didn't know the other people Sylvia and Janis had mentioned. If I saw Al, the Klan coward of the night before, I'd speak with him also. The ones I didn't know I'd try later.

I climbed the levee and walked along it until I reached the ridge at the east end of the hospital. As my eyes rose above the level of the dike, I saw an incredible expanse of water where once a quiet town had been. The water was still four feet from the top of the dike. It didn't seem to be rising.

I saw Nathan with a group of guys standing on the top of the levee about thirty feet away. He wasn't on my list, but I figured I'd start with him. I approached swiftly. They stopped talking and looked at me when I was about ten feet from them.

"Scott's looking for you," I lied.

"Something wrong with Daddy?"

"He said to come on up."

Nathan detached himself from the group and followed me.

People filled every space on the first floor of the hospital. The stairway to the second floor was empty. Halfway up the steps, I grabbed the front of his shirt and swung him around to face me.

"I want the truth out of you about what the hell you and your family have been up to."

He shoved my hand off his shirt. "Fuck you," he said, and began to walk away.

I reached around, got another fistful of his shirt, and yanked him to a stop. I rammed his back up against the wall. He squawked and tried to twist away. I slammed him again.

"Why aren't you willing to help Scott? He's your brother. If you don't love Scott now, think of how much you did as a kid, and be willing to help him out."

"You're the one accused of murder."

"You think he's going to be happy if his lover is executed or is in jail for the rest of his life?"

"I don't care."

"But he would."

He stopped struggling. I think he was surprised at my strength. I knew there was a good reason I worked out with Scott as often as I could.

"Whether you care for him or not, I need answers, and I intend to get them. Stupid as it may sound, for Scott's sake, I don't want to bring trouble to you, or your brothers and sisters, but I'm going to find out who killed the sheriff no matter who is implicated. I'm going to get my butt out of the sling it's in. I'll hurt you if I have to, and I want answers."

I let go a little. "One thing I don't get is why you hate your brother."

"Which one?"

"Huh?"

"I don't really hate Scott." He hesitated. His eyes got moist. "I just never understood, and he never came and talked to me. He just kept secrets from me. He never told me all the important stuff. I loved him. He could have talked to me. Instead, he stopped visiting. I don't hate him. I want it to be like it used to be. I guess I don't hate Hiram, but he's a good hater. He's very convincing when he wants to be. He looks out for me and the whole family."

"Did he kill the sheriff to protect your sister's honor?"

"How did you know about that?"

"Did he?"

"I don't think so."

"What was he doing illegal on his farm that the sheriff found out about?"

"Nothing half the farmers in the county aren't doing. Skimming money from the federal government price supports. Hiram just got a little greedy, is all. He's got more acres than almost anybody. Sheriff wanted a cut."

"And then this thing with your sister came along?"

"I swear, Hiram promised me they were only going to talk about it at the meeting. They were going to go to the sheriff and ask him to resign. They were going to threaten him with prosecution. I think Hiram had talked Shannon into seeing a lawyer in Macon."

The door from the first floor banged open and several kids rushed past us. I followed Nathan back outside.

I found Clara, Cody, Al Holcomb, and Wainwright Richardson just outside the entrance. Clara had her hands on her hips. Richardson was waving a finger in her face.

I walked up to them.

Richardson saw me, turned to Cody, and said, "Arrest this man."

Clara said, "No."

Cody asked, "How come you ordered him left in the jail to die and then lied to me when I asked if he was gone?"

Richardson glared at him. "You can't be accusing me of any crime. With the water rising there were a million things to think about."

I asked, "Why'd you order me arrested in the first place?"

"You need charges," Clara said. "What happened that you didn't tell me about?"

"I don't have to tell any of you anything."

Part of the crowd had formed a circle around us.

Richardson saw them and licked his lips. "We should move to a less public place."

"No," I said. "Let's talk about it with the whole town as witness. If they're going to lynch me for being gay or for killing the sheriff, then let's do it. Cut the crap and get it over with. Why did you arrest me?"

"A witness came forward who said he saw you with the sheriff in the early morning hours, just before the murder."

"Who's the witness?"

"I don't have to tell you that." He raised his voice. "Listen, you people—" he pointed at me—"this man killed the sheriff, we have a witness. Now, Cody, arrest him before the crowd gets ugly."

"No," Clara said.

Cody looked from one to the other of us. He said, "There's no jail to take him to. I talked to a few people. I was in one of the rescue boats with Everett, one of the jail guards. He said you told him to leave him to die."

"You would take the word of a black man against—" He stopped.

Angry murmurs rose from the African-American people in the crowd around us. Several people said, "Let's ask Everett."

Cody asked, "Who's the witness?"

Holcomb said, "Who's this deputy to ask questions of the man who has been coroner in this county for fifteen years?"

"Al, go put your thumb in a hole in the levee," Clara said.

A number in the crowd laughed. At least they didn't seem overtly hostile to me, and Clara and Cody were on my side.

A man in bib overalls with a snaggletooth worked his way to the front of the throng: a cliché finally come true. The guys who had threatened us at Magnolia's bar had been horrors to look at, but this guy was worse than all of them combined. He was probably only a few pounds short of being able to play half the offensive line on a pro football team. Three warts on his right cheek were putrid shades of green. A running sore on his lip gleamed redly. He was half bald, with the rest of his hair hanging dirty and stringy halfway down his back. He carried a small child in his right arm. His gray eyes met mine briefly, then turned to Richardson. "Folks here want an answer, Wainwright. 'Bout time you began speaking up. You tell us who says he saw this man with the sheriff."

"Now, Henry, you're not worried about this queer?" No angry murmurs greeted this slur from Richardson.

Henry said, "What's right is right. Is there somebody who saw him, or are you making it up?" Henry planted his feet squarely in front of Richardson. He seemed ready to wait for the next flood before he would move.

Richardson said, "Well, it's not my fault. Someone came forward. I don't have to reveal it unless it's in court. I'll talk to Judge Collins. This won't be mob rule."

"Judge evacuated yesterday morning," Henry said. "He can't get back, and we can't get out. You tell us, now."

"All right," Richardson said. "I'm revealing this under protest." He gazed at the crowd. They didn't look unfriendly, more expectant and curious at this minor spectacle.

Richardson said, "Hiram Carpenter saw him."

I realized that this was why Hiram, just before I got arrested, had been certain he wouldn't have to put up with me.

The crowd murmured and rumbled as crowds in the background of movies are wont to do. We waited while people searched for Hiram, but he was not to be found.

Finally, Henry, still holding the child, said, "Seems like you got one man's word against another."

"You going to believe an outsider?" Richardson asked.

"Don't know if I much believe anything. I know there's water in the streets and my house is probably gone. Do know this man needs to be treated according to the law."

"We'll wait for attorneys and the judge to get back," Clara said.

"Arrest him," Richardson ordered Cody.

"No," Cody said.

Richardson began to rant at Cody, then at me. He tried shoving me toward a police car. I knocked his hand away. When he reached for me again, Henry blocked him.

"Arrest Wainwright," Clara said to Cody.

"You don't have that kind of authority," Richardson said.

Clara turned her back on him. She said, "Arrest him for attempted murder."

Word of her directive spread quickly. The crowd swirled and eddied around us as they chattered and clamored with the news. Eventually, Richardson was hustled away to the back of a police car. Finally, the crowd began to disperse. I thanked Henry.

"Don't much like your kind, either," he said.

"Thank you anyway," I said.

He just nodded and harumphed and walked off.

I reentered the hospital. Trudged up the stairs to the second floor. In the CCU all was quiet. I entered the lounge. Mrs. Carpenter sat with her back to me. She had her hands folded over a tissue in front of her. She was crying.

I put my hand on her arm. "Is Mr. Carpenter okay?"

"He spoke and recognized everyone this morning."

I looked at her. Her face was deeply wrinkled around her chin and mouth. Her gray hair was pulled back, but wisps had gotten loose. I saw a bit of Scott around the eyes.

"Can I get you something?" I asked.

She sniffled. She took her hands off the tissue and placed them flat on the table.

In front of her on the tissue was a rusty razor blade with what looked like flecks of dried blood on it.

She looked down at the razor and back at me.

She spoke very softly. "One of my children is a murderer." She sighed deeply. "A parent goes through a great deal with children. Illness and worry. Tragedy and happiness. This is wrong."

"Where did you find it?"

"I gave my husband a sponge bath this morning. It was in the folds of the cuff of his pajama bottoms. It isn't his. He never uses this kind."

I sat next to her, patted her hand.

"Someone came into his room who was a murderer. At least one member of the family has been with him all that time. I've talked to the hospital personnel and my children. You haven't been in his room since you found the sheriff. You couldn't have put it there. I can't believe one of my children would do this and then try and implicate an innocent person."

I said, "Maybe one of the hospital personnel dropped it."

"No," she said. "Daddy didn't want strangers touching him. We've cared for him. I've washed his hair and given him sponge baths. My children have changed the sheets and helped him up."

I agreed it was probably one of her kids, but I couldn't absolutely rule out a doctor, nurse, or orderly.

She pulled another tissue out of her purse and wiped her eyes. "I am going to question my children about this. I will know the truth."

Nathan entered the room. "Mama, I found everybody except Hiram. They'll be along in a minute." He saw her crying. "What's wrong, Mama? This guy trying to hurt you?"

"Oh, hush, Nathan." A few minutes later, Nathan, Mary,

and Shannon stood in a circle staring at the razor blade. Mary called into the CCU and Scott came out. He sat down next to his mother.

Mrs. Carpenter told them of finding the razor blade. Shannon began to cry and slumped to the ground. Nathan caught her.

Hiram hurried in. "What's going on?" he asked.

"One of you killed the sheriff," I said.

Hiram lunged at me.

Mrs. Carpenter stood up. "Stop it!"

Everybody stopped.

Mrs. Carpenter eyed each of her children in turn. She slowly sat down. "No matter what, I want the truth."

Tears ran down Shannon's face. Her muffled sobs were the only sound in the room.

Nathan explained the situation to his brother.

Hiram said, "Anybody who came into the room could have put it there." He pointed at me. "He could have."

"He hasn't been in there since the murder," Scott said.

I said, "Hiram, why did you tell Richardson you saw me with the sheriff? You know I wasn't. You're lying."

He began to protest, but I cut him off. "I know you think it's going to be my word against yours, but I know I wasn't there. Therefore you are trying to save yourself or cover up for someone else."

Shannon burst out sobbing.

"Peter raped me!" Her voice shook with rage. "He humiliated me. He demanded I see him again. I refused. I'd stolen money from my job. They made me quit. He found out. I don't know how. I had to put a stop to that horrible man."

Scott gave me an agonized look. "I'm sorry," he said.

Hiram slammed his fist against the wall. "Shannon, don't say anything!" he commanded.

"She's got to tell the truth," Scott said.

Hiram looked like he might attack Scott.

Mrs. Carpenter said, "Y'all hush." She moved to Shannon and embraced her distraught daughter. She glanced up for a moment. "Y'all should leave now."

We left to the sound of Mrs. Carpenter murmuring to Shannon.

Three days later we said good-bye to Mr. and Mrs. Carpenter in their front parlor. The prognosis for Mr. Carpenter's full recovery was good and the Carpenter home had survived the flood unscathed. This was tempered by the arrest of Shannon for the sheriff's murder.

Todd Bristol in Chicago and a team from Atlanta had been hired by Scott to defend his sister. He had paid her bail. That morning Mrs. Carpenter had gone with her daughter to the lawyers to find out what to do next.

Shannon had barely blinked in the past few days. She had refused to speak to Scott. He had tried talking to Hiram before we left. Hiram filled the air with a string of imprecations at his brother.

"It may have been self-defense," Mrs. Carpenter told me over breakfast that morning. "That son of a bitch sure provoked her." She was the only one in the family with whom Shannon had spoken in the last three days.

Shannon had not confessed any details to her. She was strong and athletic, and certainly had the strength to drag the sheriff around. A clandestine assignation, drugs or knockout drops in a drink, lots of forests and swamps around in which to do the deed. I suspected Hiram had helped her—if not in the killing, at least in the aftermath. Putting the body in our car had certainly been aimed deliberately to ruin one, or both, of us.

Scott had spoken to a few of his contacts in the press. After he recovered, Dennis would have a job far from Brinard. We'd stopped to see him each day and we promised him a long exclusive on Scott's coming out.

One road had been opened out of town the night before. The water was receding slowly. We were headed directly for New York and appearances on news and talk shows.

Scott insisted we fly first-class so we wouldn't be bothered by tons of gawkers. After we took off, we settled down. I engrossed myself in *Dead Man's Island* by Carolyn Hart. I'd barely been able to get to sleep last night from reading it until Scott had finally ordered me to turn out the light. The book was so good it took my mind off the horrors of the past few days.

Now, Scott sat very quietly, hardly moving, mostly staring out the window. I looked up after twenty pages. Tears ran down his face. I pulled out my hanky.

"It's clean," I said as I gave it to him. I put my hand on his arm.

He wiped his eyes.

He said, "I had a long talk with Nathan yesterday. I should have years ago. I should have gone home more. I should have made them accept me. I shouldn't have let it go so long."

"What happened is not your fault."

"I should have spent more time with them. I know most of my brothers and sisters have big hangups about you and me, but that shouldn't have stopped me from going home and bringing you with. They're my family. Wrong-headed as they might be, I love them."

I held his hand for a long while. I saw his eyes begin to nod and close when suddenly he turned to me and asked, "I told you my fantasy as a kid. You didn't tell me yours. What was it?"

"When I was a kid, I dreamed of standing next to a professional baseball player. If he suddenly maybe wanted something, I'd run get it, and he'd be grateful, and he'd thank me, and he'd talk to me, and he'd take me with him everywhere he went, and we'd be best friends. At the time it wasn't a sexual fantasy, just a kid's dream."

He smiled and pulled me close and kissed me.